ALTERNATE
UNIVERSE

ALTERNATE UNIVERSE

THE PROFESSOR'S DIARIES

Dr. Ashraf R Aziz

Alternate Universe
The Professor's Diaries

Edited by:
Candice L Davis
CandiceLDavis.com

Cover illustration by the author titled, The Shell of Knowledge

ISBN 978-1-7327787-0-2

The universe and life within it are full of mysteries with so many questions to be answered. Even when some questions are answered, they generate new puzzles and mysteries, with many more questions than answers.

The brain is the most complicated device in the entire universe. Within its complex networks and connections, a vast amount of hidden information that no one understands yet. Understanding brain phenomena, like the nature of consciousness and the purpose of sleep and dreams, might be the key to understanding bigger questions, like the nature of the universe itself and what is behind it.

Curiosity, mixed with imagination and freedom from predetermined dogma, could open so many doors to discoveries, or at least open new pathways that could lead us to those discoveries.

Learning to listen to the brain allows us to access a very valuable resource of inspiration and a vast knowledge that is hidden inside the brain, yet within our reach to grasp. Unfortunately, doing so quietly has become harder to do among the hustle and bustle of daily life and the increasing disturbance of modern technology.

Our brain is like a precious torch that we need to be able to see clearly in the dark, and distraction is like a wind that blows over it and risks extinguishing its flames. In that case, we remain in the dark, lose our way, and block ourselves from accessing this precious asset that we all have.

The ideas in this book came over many years of imagination and continuous learning, in combination with living life, working and interacting with my lovely patients who taught me love and a great deal of knowledge along the way.

Some of you will find these ideas amusing, but others might see them as "unusual," but at least, my hope is for those ideas to be perceived as interesting and thought-provoking.

I want to thank my lovely family throughout the writing of this book, especially my daughters, Sherry and Caroline, who accepted talking about these ideas repeatedly, still perceived them as exciting and without complaining too much. Also, I want to thank my brother Sherif, for sharing many of these thoughts with me and taking some of them with a grain of salt, stimulating further discussions and research. I also want to sincerely thank my lovely wife, Manal, who always supported me and managed to keep me tethered tightly to this reality. Without her, I might have been floating somewhere in outer space a long time ago.

I would not have been able to do any of this without the support and the unconditional love of my family and my patients that is injected in me every day of the week, during the span of this hard but fascinating life so far.

ALTERNATE UNIVERSE

THE PROFESSOR'S DIARIES

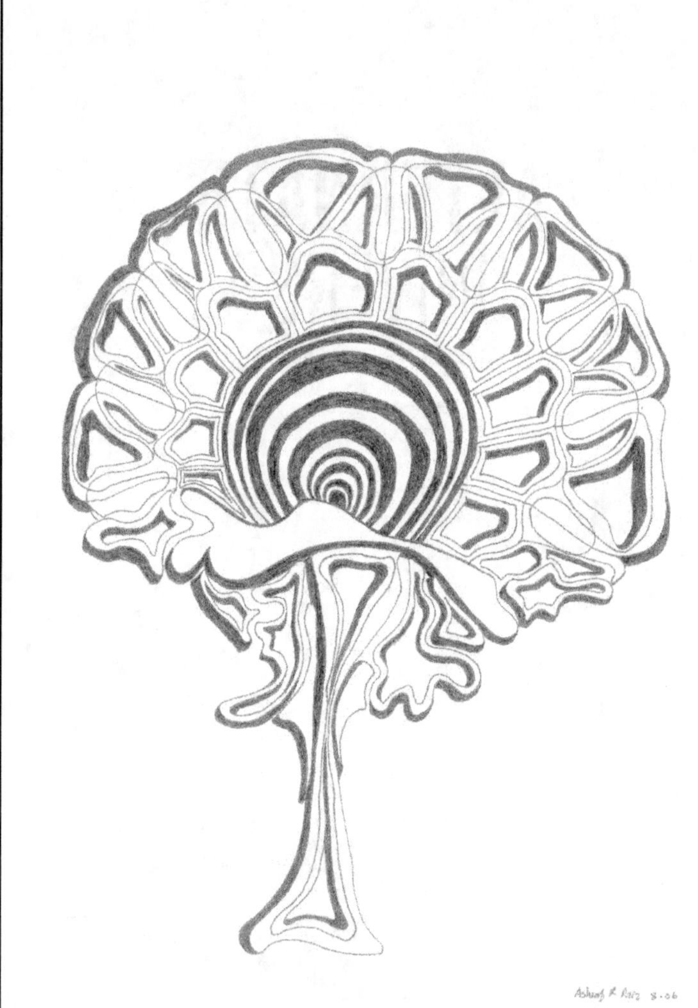

cross section of the brain tree

CHAPTER 1

Smooth Operator, the Mighty Brain

I'm Dr. Ezra Zachary, professor of neuropsychiatry and neurosurgery at the University of Toronto, School of Medicine. I have spent my entire professional career studying the brain. My journey started as an interest, that later transformed into an obsession with this incredible organ, trying to understand its many secrets and mysteries. I have seen, touched, and smelled live brains during the thousands of surgical operations that I have performed. I have also seen, felt, and smelled cadaver human and animal brains thousands more times in my research. I've dissected many cadaver brains as part of my many lectures and anatomy classes. I know the location and the function of every part of the brain and how it carries out its task.

I have seen the brain through thousands of PET scans, CT scans, and MRI scans, and I've analyzed thousands of electroencephalograms. I know the difference between healthy and unhealthy brains and normal and abnormal brain waves. I know precisely the expected pattern of brain waves that should be expressed during sleep, wakefulness, anesthesia, and various disease states.

It still amazes me when I see the brain through PET scans, showing a very avid uptake of the radioactive sugar that dwarfs any other organ in the body, including the spinal cord, and I always wonder why it is that way. No other tissue in the body gets even closer to this amount of activity. It is the mighty brain that takes the lion's share of that sugar, as if something significant and mysterious is happening there, inside our brains. This pattern can be observed in every brain PET scan, even in people with dementia.

To me, the brain is the electronic device that translates our reality for us. Through it, we see the world, and we depend on this perception one hundred percent of the time. We trust its translation, but we are not exactly sure if the brain is showing us the actual reality or a false interpretation, a reality that only exists inside the brain and has nothing to do with the external reality. Like in a scenario where a blind man is dependent on a friend to help him navigate through and see the world for him and tell him what it looks like while his friend could be giving him a modified or a completely different picture of the world.

Neuroscience tells us that the human brain is a very smooth operator, like a fancy car that we feel very comfortable inside it, even when we're driving on a bumpy, or unpaved road. It gives us a sense of continuity and smoothness to allow us to function to our best and fastest performance, but in the process, it is also deceiving us into believing that things around us are smooth and continuous, when they're not.

When I was seven years old, after I learned that the Earth was a sphere, and not flat, I wondered why people in the Southern Hemisphere don't see themselves upside down and the people at the Equator don't see themselves sideways, as it actually is, as seen from outer space? I asked many people around me at that time, but no one was able to give me a satisfactory answer. A teacher once told me, it is because the Earth is too big, and we are very tiny. Someone else said it is because of Earth's strong gravity, but I wasn't convinced. Much later in life, only a few months ago, I answered the question myself. I discovered that it is solely a function of our brain, which makes that adjustment for us automatically.

Our brain gives us those false perceptions to help us function the best we can, without delay or hesitation. Imagine perceiving an upside-down reality whenever we travel to Australia from the Northern Hemisphere. First; we would realize immediately that the Earth is a sphere, not flat. Secondly; beside jet lag, we also would get a positional lag, and would need to adjust to an upside-down reality in the new location, which may take several days to weeks to adjust— a complete waste of a few weeks in that case. But no, the brain makes this automatic adjustment for us, without our knowledge so we can function at our best with no delays and with no questions asked.

The brain also performs many other tricks for us, without our awareness. It cancels out several defects in our vision, such as the central blind spot, the site of entry or exit of the optic nerve into the eye. Otherwise, we would see a large black hole in the center of our visual field. It also flips images automatically for us; otherwise, we would see an upside-down and backward image of reality with a large hole in the center. To see the world in such a way would have been extremely inconvenient and distracting and would delay us so much. The brain also suppresses the two hundred or so, jerky saccadic eye movements we experience every minute and gives us a continuous steady image of reality; otherwise, our visual field would appear to have constant seizures.

Another essential feature that the brain also gives us is the 3D image of reality, which may not exist outside of the brain. The images we see every day, are focused flat on our retinas, just like the flat 35-millimeter film inside old cameras, or the digital light sensor inside digital cameras. Subsequently, the brain translates those 2D images for us into 3D images, again for our ultimate convenience. Imagine making love to your partner while seeing him or her in 2D, as they may truly be, how inconvenient and less exciting. Almost like making love to a life-size, living, breathing sexy Playboy magazine poster that is flat.

Information from reality, such as images, sounds, physical sensations, taste, and smell, are broken down into digital pieces. For example, images are deconstructed into vertical and horizontal lines and circles, and only in the brain, where those shapes are analyzed, and perceived as 3D images. This process is also the same for sound, touch, and all the other sensations and feelings of our surroundings. Everything is broken down, digitized, and then reanalyzed. All these perceptions happen almost simultaneously, in fractions of a second, to give us the best-perceived picture of reality, as the brain decides it should be. Similarly, colors are constructed in the brain and do not exist out there in the world. Instead, they are cooked up in the brain from mixtures of different wavelengths of colorless electromagnetic radiation.

The brain is that black box recorder that knows the truth, the whole truth, and nothing but the truth, but it is hiding everything from us. The real question is: where does it all happen and how? Where does consciousness happen, how, and when? How can bits and pieces of digitized information finally translate into an idea, a decision, or an emotion, like love or anger? All neuroscientists, including myself, were surprised by the results of what's called the "Libet experiment," which showed that we only become conscious of our actions after they have already happened, not before, as common sense tells us it should be. Decisions are made in the subconscious brain, and then we become conscious of them at least three hundred milliseconds later. We do not willingly initiate the actions; we just become aware of them after they happen.

The subjects of the experiment showed unconscious brain activity to initiate an action, like moving an arm, for example, about three hundred and fifty milliseconds before reporting the conscious decision to move. They also demonstrated an earlier crescendo rise in the potential to move as early as one and a half seconds before the action. This experiment has since been verified several times with the same results. That means the sophistication of the human brain is in analyzing what happens in the brain underneath the frontal cortex, just understanding it better and not controlling it or directing it.

If our brain is like a computer, is it a Windows or a Mac? Is the hard drive making all the decisions, or is it responding to external commands? Could it be receiving Wi-Fi signals from a nearby router and connecting to the internet directly to an external server? In that case, when we dissect the brain, we'd only examine the computer, and we wouldn't find the information or the consciousness there, because it would be outside the brain, in the server. And in that case, where would that source be, and why would it be transmitting this reality to us?

The other great mystery, which puzzled me my entire life, is the mystery of sleep and dreams. Sleep is something we all have to do every day, a state we spend roughly one-third of our lives, and still, we don't understand why we must do it, or where do we go when we sleep. What are those weird dreams, and why do we have them? Is there an alternate universe that we visit during sleep? Or a different wavelength we tune to during sleep, when we turn off the wavelength of our reality and switch the channel to another wavelength, experiencing different realities? Just like changing the TV channels using the remote control.

After all these years of studying the brain, and I am still not able to answer those questions. I only can speculate, come up with theories, or imagine to my best ability. If someone like me, with all my extensive training, couldn't answer those questions, who could? After spending all that time with the brain, practically my entire life, from anatomy to physiology, from neurosurgery to psychoanalysis, from trauma, stroke, and seizure to schizophrenia and delusions, I've seen it all, and I still can't explain this mystery. All the advances in neuroscience are achieved in the areas of anatomy, physiology, and understanding diseases, but we are still paralyzed when it comes to answering these difficult questions — the mystery of consciousness and sleep. Our increasing knowledge of the brain is like making advances in knowing our city geographically very well, all the streets, parks, highways, and buildings, without knowing where the city itself is located? Who built it, and who is governing it? I felt that answering those questions would also solve other unanswered mysteries. The simple but hard to answer questions that almost every child and many curious adults ask sometimes. Questions like, who are we? Where did we come from, and what is our purpose in this universe?

I felt very frustrated and yet compelled to understand and try to solve those mysteries. I wanted to know where my city was. Who built it? And who come every night to clean it and maintain it while I slept? The answers, I believed, could be surprisingly very simple and straightforward. We sleep every night, and we really could and should understand what happens there. We think of ourselves as conscious beings, most of the time at least, and we should be able to understand what that means and where and when does it happen inside the brain?

On the other hand, if it is coming from an outside source, what is the nature of that source, where is it located and why it is doing so? How we get ideas from electrical signals in multiple neurons. I was sure that, if we look close enough with an open mind, we would be able to connect the dots, like a smart detective who can put facts together to solve a mystery or at least come up with a plan or a theory and try to prove it experimentally.

I tried to use the resources of the university to find the answers. I used my research capabilities, and relied on other researchers in the field, and searched in other departments, such as cosmology, physics, chemistry, biology, computer science, and of course, the mother of all nonsense, philosophy. I kept this secret to myself all the time, walking around with all these ideas and intentions inside my head circling constantly. Until six months ago, I met Sarah, a postgraduate research fellow in neuroscience. A brilliant and beautiful woman in her mid-twenties, from a second-generation immigrant Russian family. Sarah had a high level of knowledge in many different fields of science, mixed with an unbelievable enthusiasm to learn and a great ability to analyze and integrate new information. Sarah gave me another dimension of thoughts about so many things. Before Sarah (B.S.), my theories did not include love in the equations. As science and scientists always do, I ignored love, but I found that my theories were incomplete. After Sarah (A.S.), my theories changed significantly. I saw another dimension, another wavelength that I hadn't seen or been aware of before, and these changed my scientific views and methods dramatically. Sarah helped me intellectually, in formulating many ideas. Putting to use her prior studies as a major in theoretical physics, she extended a significant dimension of knowledge to mine, a perspective that I was missing. Sarah turned my theories upside down as she later turned my life upside down as well.

I promised myself to try my best to decode the mystery of consciousness and sleep and subsequently decode other mysteries, like the secret of life, our origin, and the origin of the universe. I also promised myself that nothing would stop me from knowing the truth at any cost, and I would stop at nothing to get there. I would do anything, collaboration in research, experimental human research (unethical, well, ok with me), animal research, cheating, lying, stealing data, and even crime if necessary. I became addicted to a drug called "Finding the truth," and just like an addict, I would do anything to get the drug I am seeking at any cost. The only difference is that there is no rehab program existing to treat this type of addiction. Similarly, just like any other sort of addiction, it could become life-threatening in the end, in a fatal episode of pleasure.

In my late forties, I felt, I did not have much time left before my own brain would start to degenerate, as well as my body, and I would become a useless file in the recycle bin folder on a computer screen somewhere. I had to hurry up.

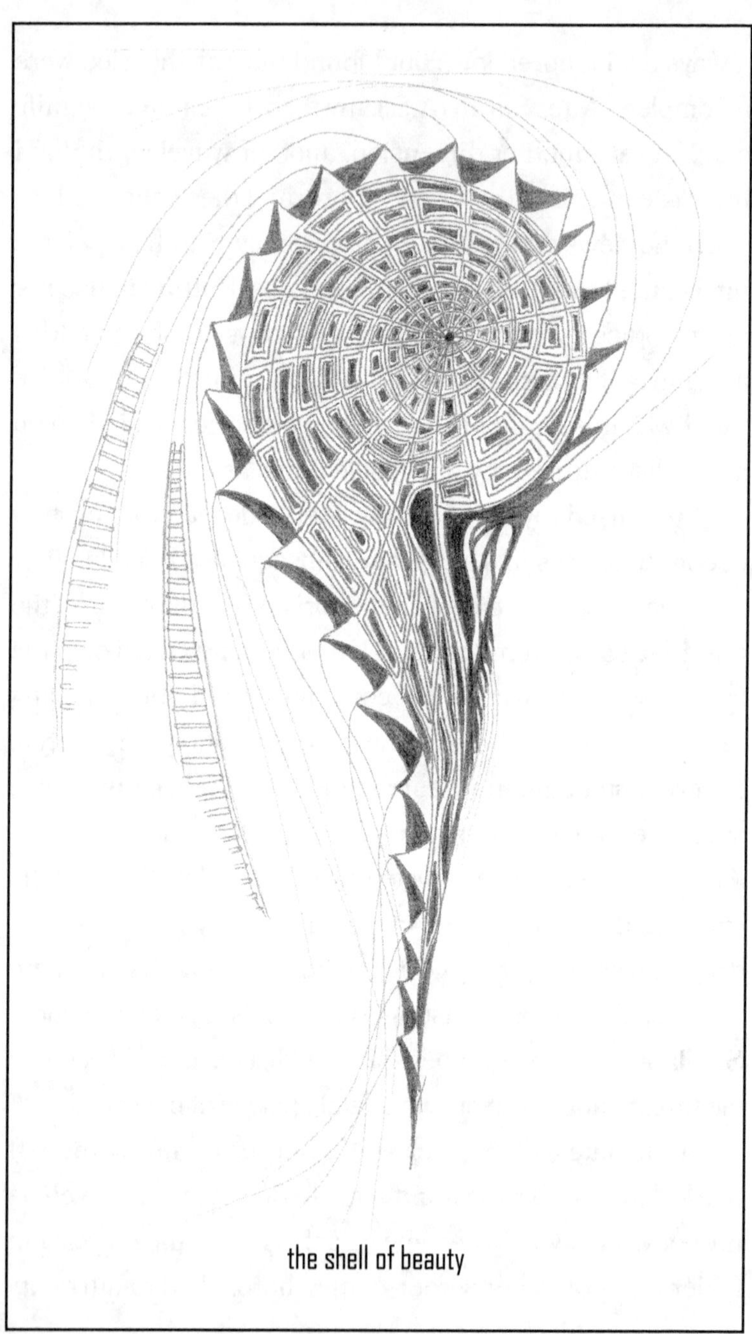

the shell of beauty

CHAPTER 2

What does it mean to be human?

In the operating room, drilled a hole in the thick skull bones with an electric bone drill specially made to cut the cranial bones. I removed a plate of skull bone, opened the cranial cavity, peeled off the membranes covering the brain, first the dura mater, the arachnoid, and then the most intimate pia mater. Then I saw the soft white brain, beneath my fingers. I was looking at that living device that controls everything in the body, the machine that makes us move and feel everything around us. The ultimate source of our creativity, emotions, and personality. The device that defines who we are. I had a face-to-face interaction with that mysterious, living, biological, electronic device, the mighty brain. I only saw and felt a white, soft material, like rice pudding, but one that possesses the most fantastic extraordinary capabilities, compared to any device in the whole universe. It was almost like touching inside a supercomputer made of white Gel.

The patient's body laid on the operating table, under deep anesthesia, did not appear to me to be alive, or even a human at all. He looked the same as the operating table. I looked at the anesthesiologist, and he indicated to me that the patient was ready, totally out; his brain waves did not show any activity.

The operation was indicated to remove a malignant tumor from the frontal lobe of the brain. During the surgery, the patient suddenly became critically distressed. His vital signs became unstable. Holding his brain in my hands, I watched it turning greyish, from a pinkish white color earlier. I knew the significance of the emergency when I noticed the color change; the brain was becoming hypoxic or anoxic on us. It meant that this man might not return to be the same as he was before the operation. He could lose a function or some memories or experience a change of personality. That had happened to a few of my patients before, and I hated to see it occur. Fortunately, finally, the patient's vital signs returned to stable, and his brain regained good circulation and changed to pink again, and I was able to breathe a sigh of relief.

When the patient woke up, he was able to tell me about his experiences, feelings, and thoughts. I examined him, and I felt that he was back to human again. I wondered what was that valuable asset that he lost temporarily during the operation, his consciousness? On the operating table, the patient was no more conscious than a living tree, but later, after he woke up, he was back to living as a human again. When we die, we become like a dead tree, but under anesthesia, we become like a living tree. We lose that consciousness forever at death; we become permanently under anesthesia, without recovery, and the body that I operated upon becomes like a jacket that was taken off and thrown on the ground, lifeless.

I perform my operations and all my medical skills on people's temporary jackets. Therefore, I should not be upset if I make a mistake or a patient dies or loses functions because I only made a mistake on the jacket, just like a tailor who ruined a dress, an expensive dress, yes, but still a dress after all. There is much more in people than their physical bodies. The body is almost like any physical object, it could be a table, a car, a radio, or a computer, but with life, it becomes something else, something conscious, with feelings, pain and emotions, personality, preferences, and willpower, among other unseen dimensions that are much more meaningful and deeper than the physical self.

Inside every living being, and especially humans, there is that unseen deep and boundless well, without a bottom, with limitless possibilities and potential, an infinite wealth of information and resources.

We are limited but contain the unlimited. Our bodies bound us, but deep inside us, there is access to the infinite, boundless reality. We are timely, but within us, there is access to the timeless.

I wondered what the difference was between this patient of mine and a robot with very high artificial intelligence. Supercomputers had become very smart and could surpass humans in knowledge and trivia. IBM had built a computer that was able to beat Kasparov (the best chess player at that time), many years ago. The Watson supercomputer, also developed by IBM, was able to beat the top players at the *Jeopardy* trivia game most of the time. Was it possible that these supercomputers could replace me as a doctor in the future? Indeed, supercomputers could become super-doctors in diagnosing diseases and recommending the best therapy available. They could be much better than human doctors, without the interference of emotions, personal bias, social, cultural influences, and personal gains. But indeed, a robot or a computer doctor would be a very cold doctor, one I would hate to treat me. Patients need doctors who know their illnesses well but who also can feel some of their pain and hold their hands in genuine understanding, telling them, "I will help you no matter what happens, and I will never give up on you." A computer doctor cannot do that.

Could a computer become a compassionate doctor? Very unlikely.

Could a computer become creative and artistic? I thought not, as this would require a different thought process, a simple switch in function, but not possible to achieve.

The computer gets information from the past and can make intelligent decisions for the present and the future, but it cannot create art, cannot design a creative building or a structure or a statue, even silly ones like those we see in contemporary art museums. Only a human can do that, and that is why we appreciate that art and display it in museums because it has our human signature.

Could a computer become an addict? Inject himself with heroin, for example? I thought again, unlikely. To become addicted, we need the beautiful brain. We need the brain reward pleasure centers connected with emotions and feelings that follow acts of pleasure. I was sure that supercomputers could not feel pleasure even if the wiring were correct. The computer can solve complex cognitive functions, but cannot be compassionate, nor creative, and cannot become an addict. To become an addict, you need to be human, or at least an animal with a brain that has pleasure centers. Experimentally, some animals were turned into addicts for pleasurable things, like sex, food, and drugs.

What makes us humans are not the intelligence or cognitive ability; it is the feelings, emotions, and compassion, the hate crimes, the silly stuff, jealousy, envy, feelings of love and affection — the fear, anxiety, worry, and of course, addiction. You must be fully human to be an addict.

We are as human as our psychological disorders are, and how much love we have; those are the things that define us as humans. A very sophisticated robot of the future will not feel love, cannot become an addict, and will not be able to make love to anyone or satisfy anyone sensually, sexually, or emotionally. The hidden dimensions of love, affection, and creativity are our hallmarks as humans. Historically, we became humans when we started to be creative and artistic without direct benefits to our survival. At some point in our evolution, we started drawing on cave walls, painting art, wearing exquisite jewelry, and appreciating music and dance, and that was the time when we became humans. Animals share our same DNA, and the same exact proteins, chemistry, and biology but are not creative, cannot feel art, as far as we know. They are only concerned with their survival.

Seeking art and creativity by early humans happened spontaneously and with no evolutionary incentive or a physical gain. It was just a consequence of early humans' growing brain size. As our brains increased in size, art and creativity surfaced from it spontaneously without an apparent reason.

The same is true for many contemporary artists, who feel an impulse to produce art without an incentive, just for the sake of love for art itself and without expecting much gains from it. They may not object if material gains come along the way, but it is not their primary focus. On the contrary, sometimes, pursuing art could be a detriment to some artists that negatively affect them and their families. Some artists live poor and die poor because they are so intent on seeking art, without any survival benefits to them and their families and against the survival rules of nature.

Human creativity is spontaneous, for the love of art, and is not concerned with earning money or power. It's often a spontaneous, compelling expression of art and love. Once money gets in the way, artists start to lose their creativity. Money cannot buy creativity or love. This point onward marked the dawn of human origin, creativity. When we became creative, we started to be humans.

There is also unexplained creativity, art, and beauty in all of life and nature. Beauty of unexplained reason exists everywhere in nature, in the wings of a butterfly, in the design and colors of fish and birds. They all display intrinsic artistic patterns that don't help them to survive. On the contrary, those patterns could make them weaker; beautiful, yes, but weaker and more vulnerable.

Evolution tells us that beauty might have been naturally selected because of sexual choices, as a sign of health and fitness, but that begets the next question; why does life choose to select for beauty to start with, rather than, for example, muscle strength or body size? In a different world, maybe what we consider ugly, could have been selected for as a sign of health and resilience, and not beauty.

Furthermore, there is also a significant degree of intrinsic beauty in the symmetrical structure of minerals and stones. We always think of crystals and stones as static and unchanging structures, but some gemstones, like Alexandrite, for example, change colors throughout the day, bluish-green by daylight and red by night. Other gems are known to change color with heat and pressure, and hence human emotions. So, in a sense, they are interactive with us without possessing known feelings or thoughts of their own.

Beauty and love are everywhere in nature, inside and outside of us, without a clear explanation for their existence from a Darwinian evolution point of view. I felt that there must be another driver for our evolution, other than the famous concept of "Survival of the fittest," that was introduced by Charles Darwin. A dimension of beauty, art, love, and love of beauty exists everywhere in life and nature, not based on physical survival alone. The wings of the butterfly didn't have to be that beautiful, and those precious stones that inspire us and react to our emotions didn't have to be that beautiful either.

Besides, I'd learned throughout my medical experience, over many years now, that every human has a unique print on his or her own. There is no ordinary man or woman. Everyone is unique, with his private black box, a mystery of his own. What is going on in there, in every brain, is a total secret. But unlike a black box recorder, we wouldn't know what's going on inside it, even if we opened it and analyzed it. The feelings, thoughts, beliefs, taboos, likes, and dislikes are all unique to that individual and are not shared with anyone else, even with his or her most intimate person. It is all hidden behind the facade of his or her face.

Our face and body are just like curtains that cover background activity behind the scenes, just like theatre curtains that hide the acting crew before they open for the performance. Like a beautiful dress that is hiding a body full of scars, lacerations, and possibly, beauty. Our everyday appearance in public is a theatrical performance. Only the insane, crazy, true psychopaths, or people under the influence of drugs, who cannot, or do not care to hide their true identity. Otherwise, normal humans remain obscure and mysterious forever. Every human is a unique universe on his or her own. Every time I lose a patient, I always remember him or her and portray him or her in my mind. I realize that he or she was unique, a smile, a laugh, a gesture, comments, and thoughts, all unique to them and them only. I feel sad that I'll never see that smile again; It belonged only to that person, and it is gone with his passing forever, not to be replicated ever again.

My patients amazed me every day. Every patient and every story was unique. If you build biological robots, emotions could come along and change everything along the way.

In a recent experiment using FcMRI, (Functional connectivity MRI), neuroscientists discovered that every individual has a unique connectivity pattern, a unique brain whorl, a brain-print so to speak, that can be used to identify individuals, just like fingerprints. This unique feature is based on each person's own experience and how it shaped his brain differently. Everyone has a unique fingerprint, unique ear shape, unique eye print, and unique DNA pattern, even in identical twins, and a unique brain whorl and connectivity pattern, an individual brain-print. This uniqueness stems from unique thoughts, emotions, and beliefs that only happened in a particular combination, and hence, a unique brain connectivity pattern emerged for that specific person. It's like a human print, impossible to copy, even if we made a clone of the person based on his genetic code, we would not be able to replicate his thoughts and emotions. A clone of Albert Einstein might turn out to be schizophrenic. A clone of Pope John Paul might turn out to be a fanatic terrorist, and a clone of Marilyn Monroe might turn out to be a faithful, shy housewife.

It seems that the DNA is the servant of our behavior, in interaction with our environment, and it can change through epigenetics to make whatever we want, happen for us and stays in the DNA code. It is not the master of our behavior but the servant of it. When we clone the DNA, we clone the servant, not the master, and it will have a new master to serve in the new clone. On the other hand, genes are for-ever. They transmit themselves through millions of years, sometimes unchanged, across different species. We share fifty percent of the same genes as bananas, sixty percent with the fruit fly, and ninety-eight percent with chimps. The DNA serves as a reference or a manufacturer's man-ual that resides in every cell in our bodies, around thirty trillion of them. Each cell carries its manual inside it. How remarkable! Imagine a car or a refrigerator that has a very tiny manual inside every little part of it.

The DNA serves as a resource, like references in a school library. The students come and go, but the references remain the same. In our case, the references are inside the students, not in the library, and there are thirty trillion cop-ies in each student. You could say, references are us. That's how relevant these references are. We're walking around with thirty trillion copies of our reference manuals. A very efficient way of building complicated things, like machines, cars, or robots, but self-sustained. Each one of us has a manual to build the physical body from scratch inside each of our cells. But the person is much more than that physical body. We are the end products of so many things, and effects like the environment, culture, society, parenthood, personal historical events, country of origin, our emotions, emotions of close family members and friends, education, thoughts, knowledge, and many other small things.

Even if we copy a person's DNA, we only copy the physical part, but it will not copy the person, or the brain-print, or the love inside that person. Love is a different dimension that is not coded for and has no codes to copy or manufacturer's manual to follow. Factored in, it should change all the equations and theories. That is what is lacking in science. We have ignorance when it comes to explaining the nature of love, primarily, because scientists don't want to factor it in their equations. We never read about love in science books, and yet, it's everywhere in life and nature. Furthermore, there are also more dimensions to everything around us; there are more dimensions to the rose than its physical matter and aroma; the ocean, more than its contents of water and salt; the trees, more than their wood and leaves, the wind, the ocean waves, rocks, crystals, and even atoms. There is that unseen dimension that fills all these things with meanings beyond simple explanations based on their physical matter alone.

"We live in a fantasy world, a world of illusions.
The great task in life is to find reality."

Iris Murdoch

CHAPTER 3

Mademoiselle X and Solipsism

My nurse called for, Mademoiselle X, the first patient to be seen that morning in the outpatient neuropsychiatry clinic, but the patient didn't answer. Her family responded and asked her to stand up and follow the nurse, which the young girl did exactly so but in a robotic manner. As the nurse took her medical history and vitals, there was very little response from her, as if the questions were for someone else, other than herself. I stepped inside the exam room to see the patient, along with Sarah, who had been shadowing me in the clinic for several months. Mademoiselle X was small, only five-feet-two, and extremely malnourished. She extended her arm without resistance for blood pressure measurement, but never looked at the reading. She showed no resistance to any orders but also no response. She was pale and frail, her blood pressure was low, and her pulse was feeble and fast as she seemed to be severely dehydrated.

I asked her, "What is going on?"

She said, "Nothing is going on at all, absolutely nothing; I'm not sure why I'm here."

I replied, "You are here because you're neglecting yourself to the point of wasting away. Why are you doing that to yourself?"

She said, "I'm not neglecting myself. I don't exist in the first place, and I don't need to nourish a body that I don't have. I do not have a physical body."

I asked her, "But who is that in the mirror, and whose hand and body are these?"

She answered, "I don't know who she is, but she has nothing to do with me. I've never existed. I'm not sure what those figures are or who they belong to. The mirror isn't showing true reality."

I discussed the case with Sarah and later discussed it with the patient's parents. Mademoiselle X was suffering from a medical condition called Cotard's delusion, also known as walking corpse syndrome, a very rare mental disorder that makes patients think they do not exist or have already died a long time ago. Patients affected by this disorder believe that they don't need to eat, as they are already dead or non-existent. In the case of Mademoiselle X, she believed that she had never existed at all from the start.

This disease results from a neuronal disruption in a center in the brain called the fusiform face recognition area of the brain, which allows us to recognize faces, and another error in the amygdala, the center which associates emotions to those recognized faces. When patients look at themselves or look in the mirror, they do not associate the images they see with themselves. Treatment can be attempted using antidepressants or antipsychotic medications, but it's challenging to get patients to respond to treatment. Behavioral therapy usually does not help, as these beliefs are deeply rooted and seem very real to the delusional patient.

The patient's mother asked, "Can you sedate her and insert a feeding tube in her stomach and force-feed her to save her life?"

I answered, "Absolutely not. Your daughter's body is her private temple, and she is the only person who should determine what goes into it, and what goes out, and when. This kind of force-feeding, or force anything, has never worked in medicine. Her brain will reject that food in one way or another, even if we force it inside her. It's better to try to change her thoughts first. I'll try antidepressants and behavioral therapy."

Reviewing the strange case of Mademoiselle X with Sarah reminded me of a concept I once came across known as solipsism. Solipsism is the philosophical idea that only one's mind is sure to exist and anything outside of it is of questionable existence or possibly non-existent. Things only exist in the mind, as knowledge, data, or ideas, and nowhere else. As once said before, in the famous Rene Descartes quote, "I think; therefore, I am."

Solipsism was impossible to refute or disprove in philosophical arguments and therefore could not be ruled out as a fact.

On the other hand, idealism refers to everything as ideas, thoughts, or possibly in modern science, information, or digital codes with no physical existence.

Mademoiselle X was a living example of solipsism, or perhaps idealism. In her mind, she did not have a physical body; she was only an idea, and an idea did not need physical nourishment.

As we discussed the case, Sarah commented, "I sometimes wonder, if mentally ill patients with delusions, like people with schizophrenia or mentally challenged patients, are seeing a true reality that we aren't seeing. What if they're just granted that privilege to see a truth that's hidden from us? Besides, who's to say that our reality is not the delusion and their reality is the true one? And we call them crazy. We're the crazy ones in their eyes too. Moreover, we try to give them drugs to force them to return to our illusionary reality."

I replied, "Yes if we could tap into their brains and try to see what they perceive, we might be able to explore that true reality that they see, whatever it is."

"At least we should treat them with respect," Sarah said, "And give them the benefit of the doubt. They could potentially tell us the truth about our universe. They may be seeing who built it, who is behind all this, or who could be actively communicating with them without our knowledge. On the other hand, is it possible that psychosis could have resulted from a program error or a glitch that allows them to see the true reality that is normally hidden from people with normal, everyday reality brains? An unintentional glitch in the program that opens their eyes to see true reality."

"We need to see what they see, and hear what they hear, and judge for ourselves," I told Sarah.

That morning, I had a feeling that Sarah wanted to know my secrets. I felt that she was equally interested in knowing the things I wanted to know. Sometimes, I liked to talk to her, but at other times, I felt afraid that she already knew too much about me and what I wanted to do. Overall, I found in her a challenging and curious mind with which I could share ideas and thoughts about neuroscience, physics, and life in general. I also felt that she found in me a good source of knowledge and information. With her theoretical physics background, she opened a window of information that I needed to complete my theories and allowed me to work on a plausible experiment that could lead both of us to discover the actual reality.

Whenever Sarah and I got together, I felt, many doors opened, so many projects could be created and so many possible outcomes generated in very little time. It was like a meeting between two curious minds, and the net result was much more than two. It was endless. Endless thought experiments and endless pathways branching out to find quick answers, almost like a quantum computer. Sarah always came to me for questions about the brain and neuroscience, and I went to her for questions about physics and molecular science. The merging of these two sciences in our relationship brought together two distant mountains that would have never met otherwise.

I thought as I was sharing ideas with Sarah, "Modern science has become so specialized that it is rendered ineffective by too much detailed information in one dimension, a vertical depth, without putting it all together with the big picture. If advancements in individual specialties were put together with other discoveries from other fields, it would make much better sense. Scientists are losing this connectivity between different fields of science, and so, failing to discover so many potentially connected ideas. There had to be a new science that specializes in connecting discoveries from different specialties and fields, like physics, chemistry, biochemistry, biology, genetics, astronomy, astrophysics, all medical specialties, and especially neuroscience. The old and new information had to be put together every time, in a new and independent manner, to try to answer those questions, again and again."

Sarah told me one time, when scientists were building LIGO, (The Laser Interferometer Gravitational-Wave Observatory) to detect cosmic gravitational waves, in Louisiana, they didn't allow people within twelve feet of the detectors because of humans' strong magnetic gravitational effect that could interfere with the detection process and disturb the results. As Sarah was revealing this information to me, I thought, "Why is this information hidden from doctors? This strong magnetic property of humans can certainly be used for medical purposes." I imagined all the practical uses, such as designing specific machines that could diagnose different diseases, like cancer, and opening an opportunity for new diagnostic and treatment options using electromagnetism, other than the usual surgical and pharmacologic options. I felt there is a great wealth of untapped potential for applied physics in medicine, in diagnosis, prevention, and treatment that still yet to be discovered.

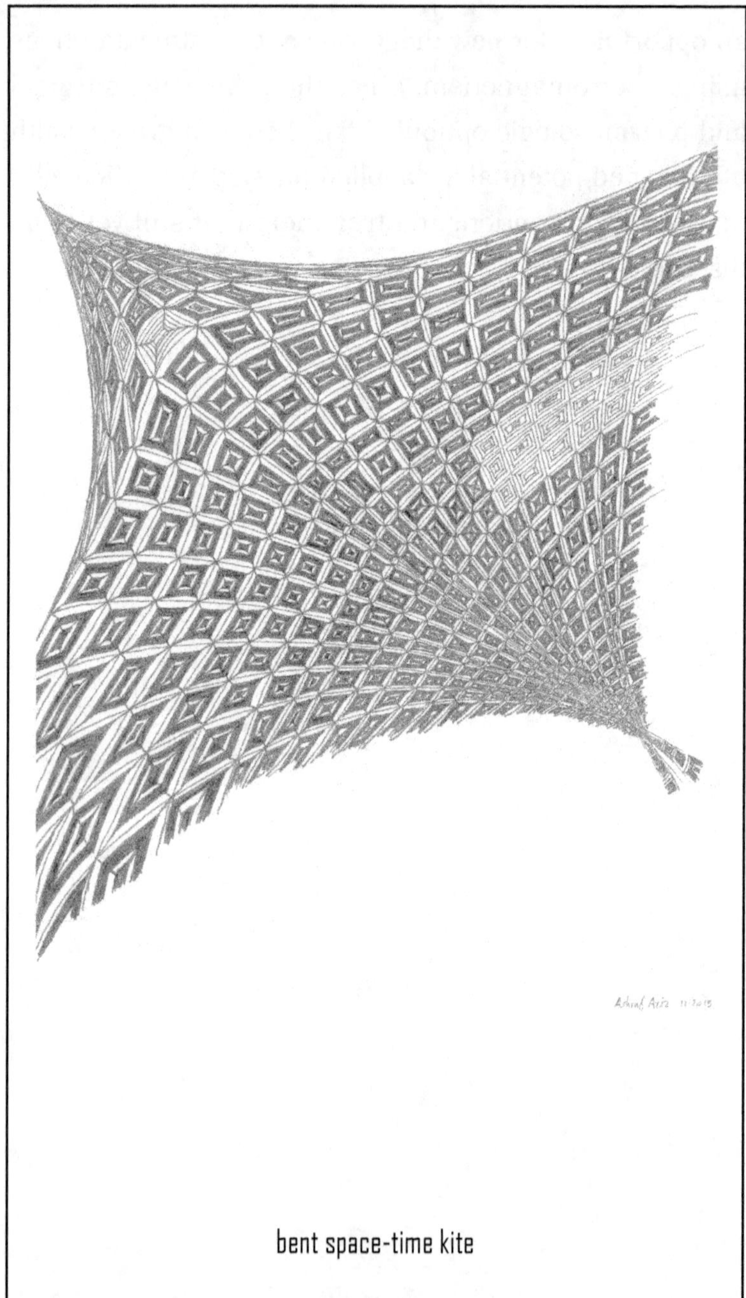

bent space-time kite

"We do not see things as they are,
we see them as we are."
Anais Nin

CHAPTER 4

Idealism versus Realism

After work, on a Friday night in spring, Sarah and I attended a lecture at the department of philosophy at our university. I had always hated philosophy because it always led to nowhere. I saw it as a jargon of words, circling around and around, and going back to where it started. To me, it was a waste of time and a waste of mental energy. I agreed to go because Sarah wanted to attend. I wanted to know her thoughts about these things, and I did not tell her my opinion on philosophy beforehand.

The seminar was about the nature of reality in ancient history, focusing on Greek philosophy. As usual, I added my thoughts at every juncture of the lecture.

The speaker started the seminar by saying, "At every period of world history, philosophers and theologians have asked the question; Is there an underlying reality that is eternal, immovable and unchanging? The ancient Egyptians believed as Hermes, (formerly known as Thoth, the God of knowledge and wisdom in ancient Egypt) taught that reality is not on Earth. Nothing on Earth is real. There are only appearances, and appearances are the supreme illusion."

The speaker continued to elaborate, "Two opposing principles have later emerged, idealism versus realism. Idealism believes that nothing, including physical stuff, has independent existence on its own, but all things are constructs of the mind and are only ideas or made of ideas. Realism, on the other hand, proposed that matter and its phenomena are the only reality, and everything can be explained from there, including the mind. Plato promoted idealism from his teacher Socrates. He gave an example in his famous book, *"The Republic"* in chapter seven, with the allegory of the cave scenario. He imagined three prisoners chained in a cave. The prisoners were tied to rocks from behind. Their arms and legs were bound and their heads were tied, so that they couldn't look at anything but a stone wall in front of them. Those prisoners had been there since birth and have never seen anything else outside of the cave. Behind the prisoners was a fire, and between them and the fire, there was a raised walkway. People outside the cave always walked along this walkway to go to the village market, carrying things on their heads like animals, plants, wood, and other goods. When people walked along the walkway, the prisoners saw their shadows and the shadows of the objects they were carrying, cast on to the cave wall in front of them. Since those prisoners have never seen the real objects before, they believed that the shadows of the objects were real. Plato suggested that the prisoners began a game of guessing what those shadows represent and which shadows would appear next."

He continued to say, "Then one day, one of the prisoners escaped from the cave and went outside. After being blinded by the bright lights outside of the dark cave, he was shocked to see the real world outside the cave. As he became used to his new surroundings, he realized that his former views of the shadows and the guessing game, he and his fellow prisoners played before were practically useless. Essentially, his former perception of reality was not accurate and incomplete. One day, the prisoner returned to the cave to inform the other prisoners of his findings, but they did not believe him and threatened to kill him if he tried to set them free."

As the speaker was going on, it came to me how ideas evolved during history, based on the thoughts of a few philosophers, and contributed to shaping the world we live in today.

The speaker then eluded further, "During Plato's lifetime, and after his death, Aristotle, his student, turned the pendulum in the opposite direction. Aristotle argued in favor of realism, founding the basis of science. He was later referenced, for the importance of the scientific method and its importance in understanding how physical matter and everything is made of and expand knowledge from there onward.

The immediate product of Aristotle's materialistic teachings was, not surprisingly, Alexander the Great. In 343 BC, King Philip II hired Aristotle to tutor the thirteen-year-old Alexander and later produced the ultimate materialist in the history of mankind, Alexander the Great, who created a vast empire that was unparalleled in size and power in all human history.

As the lecture went on, I shared some of my thoughts with Sarah along the way; I told her, "I am confident that this would not have happened if Plato had been the tutor for Alexander instead of Aristotle. Alexander would not have had this great ambition to acquire all those nations. What was he thinking? What were his reasons? Why all that interest to control and dominate, and acquire all that material stuff?

The other surprise in history was the acquisition of materialism by the early Catholic Church. Thomas Aquinas followed Aristotle's ideas and supported his views of astronomy and science and used the cosmological argument to prove the existence of God. The early church supported science, but as long as science supported the church ideology, and could not accept any other ideas, even when proved different by science. For example, it endorsed science when it said that the earth is the center of the solar system and the center of the universe and fought the scientists who later discovered that the Earth orbits around the Sun and not vice versa. The Church rejected any challenge to those fixed beliefs and ideas, as discoveries emerged through the hands of Galileo Galilei and his contemporaries because the Church didn't want to shake this foundation at any cost. The Church did not want to accept that the Earth was not the center of the universe, and forcefully persecuted whoever claimed that to be the case. Since then, our place in the universe had become more and more peripheral. We lost our special location at the center of the universe and pretty much everywhere else.

I would have expected the early Church to have taken idealism as a doctrine, over realism. I expected spiritual teachings to rise above materialism and use that to seek an ideal reality beyond this fake material reality. All major religions preach that we should avoid materialism in life and look forward to an afterlife that has a nonphysical reality.

If only idealism had persisted beyond Plato, if Aristotle had not existed or if he existed but carried out and continued the beliefs of his teacher. If the early Church followed the mystics and Gnostics' thoughts, for example, if they had followed Saint Valentinus (the third-century Roman saint and teacher) and embraced his philosophy instead of Saint Aquinas's philosophy. If Saint Aquinas did not take Aristotle's ideas to the max, or if the early Church didn't follow St Aquinas's ideology in that regard, the world would have been entirely different. The western world would have been idealistic, mystic, spiritual, and non-materialistic, turning away from the lust of matter and far from the temporary joys of the material world.

However, on the other hand, the disadvantages of that hypothetical scenario would have been missing out on the industrial and scientific revolutions that shaped the world we live in today. After all, I prefer our current situation over the opposite scenario, as we had acquired a sophisticated scientific background and understood our world better and knew our place in the cosmos better, which may not have happened otherwise.

But now, the time had come to put the modern science we acquired recently together with those prior ideas in history and philosophy and the previously available knowledge to better understand the whole picture and depart a little from the historical path. It is good that we know how we got here today, but it is best to go back in time, understand the alternative ideas in history and try to revive them based on the new scientific discoveries.

Sitting side by side next to Sarah in the lecture hall, I felt like a student again. I felt chemistry forces attracting us together. Hidden hydrogen bonds were developing in between our bodies and our brains and were commanding us to do something about it. An invisible force of attraction that I could not resist. Then a quick flashback of my life appeared in my mind for a few seconds. I was sitting in this same lecture hall around twenty-five years ago. Then, I was not paying any attention to who was sitting next to me. I was always looking forward, pressured to learn, and achieve. The brain was my only passion. Now, I felt more open to discovering love. This has never happened to me before.

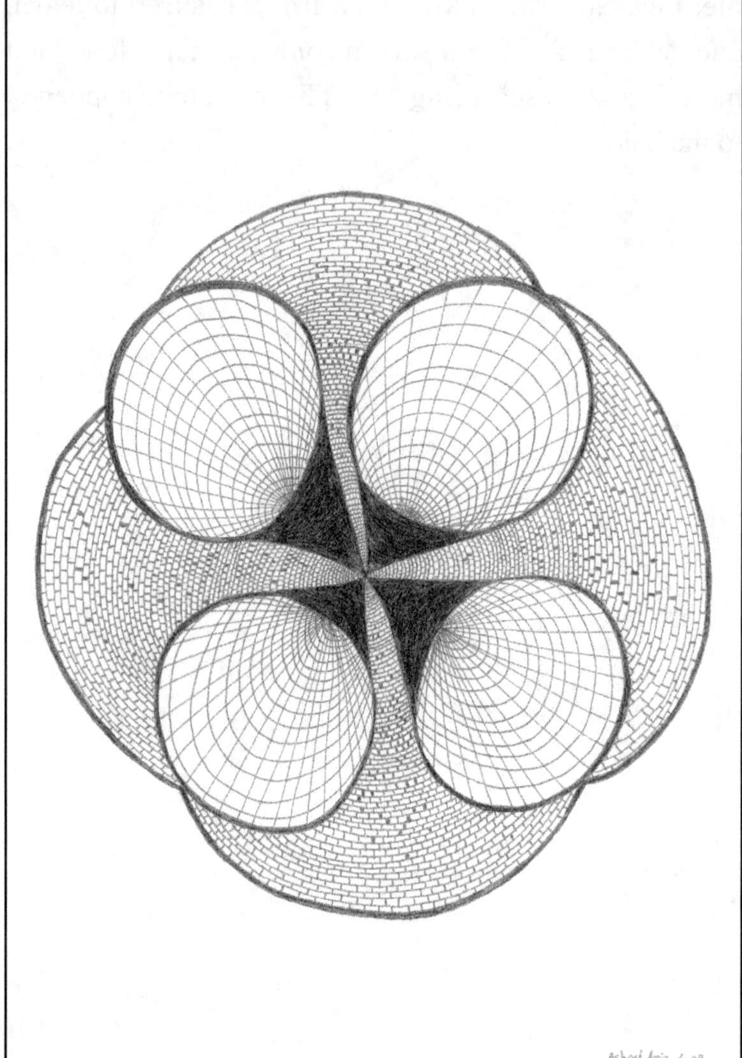

landing of the space shuttle Endeavor

CHAPTER 5

It's Not Chemistry, My Love; It's Electromagnetism

At the end of the philosophy lecture, Sarah and I walked outside the lecture hall. I asked her to join me for dinner to chat about what we'd heard in the seminar. We walked outside in the fresh air, to a nearby restaurant just outside the university campus.

I thought to myself, "I've been involved so long with my projects, and I've mostly forgotten that there is a beautiful life out here." I looked at the students, laughing, playing, and embracing each other in a lovely way, full of life.

"Why had I never done that before? Is it too late for me? Did I miss out on the good things in life? Would someone kiss me or even love me at this level and stage of my life? A distinguished professor, on the older side of age, feeling like a delayed teenager. Should I even try?"

It all seemed too good to miss; after all, I had all those theories about life and love, and I hadn't experienced either in a practical sense. I was overdue to feel love, overdue to love, and be loved. Immediately, my attention went to Sarah, this extraordinary beautiful being who shared my thoughts and interests. I thought to myself, "Would she share my love too? I must be worthy of winning her love, and I need to be very careful. I'd never really opened my feeling and myself to a woman before. What could I say and do to attract her attention without offending her? Would she respond to me? Would she be surprised and start to avoid me? Would I lose her completely if I share my feelings with her? I can't risk that for sure. I will never find anyone else so beautiful and so smart to share my thoughts. However, I want her to share something even more precious than thoughts. I want to share this love with her." And I wondered what love would feel like with Sarah. I expected it must be beautiful like her, even the slightest thought of it made me shiver. I continued to think, "I had been missing out on lots of beautiful things in life, and I am overdue. I must try to do this as soon as possible. I don't want to go on with my life without trying. I want to experience love with you, Sarah."

I told myself, "Without that love, my theories are incomplete, just trash, a waste. Isn't that what scientists are doing all along, ignoring love and avoiding understanding it, avoiding putting it in their equations with other theories of life, even though it keeps showing up and sticking out everywhere? Experiencing love with Sarah would put the finishing touches on my theories, and without it, they would never be complete. I need her love, and urgently, to complete my scientific agenda; otherwise, that agenda would be useless, and I would also be useless in that case. Her love is what will make me worthy in this world. I hope she wouldn't get offended if she knew that I need her love to finish my theories."

I decided, "I must not tell her any of this at all. She must not suspect that I am using her and her love to complete my theories. For now, I would pretend that I love her with no goals in mind. Because of love itself and because I do feel this love, and not for any other reasons and I am open to face any consequences that this love would bring. Even if it shuts down my theories or gets me expelled from the university, her love is worth it and above all things combined."

"Am I crazy? Am I experiencing a midlife crisis? But who cares?" I thought. "She is here, and she is beautiful, and I love her. Now, I am convinced. This love experience is my new challenge. How will I start? I need to be smart and clever about it."

Suddenly, I saw everything more beautiful, the trees, the flowers, the fountain with the colorful fish swimming in the water, the students, the children playing. "What a beautiful life we have. With Sarah walking beside me in this beautiful world, I wouldn't need anything else. I don't care about success or failure. I do not care if I suffer or not; nothing else is important. The only thing that is important to me is this precious, beautiful moment. It is worth eternity and is above matter and time. Nothing could ruin it, nothing from the past, present, or the future."

I said, "It's a beautiful evening."

"Yes," Sarah said, "The seminar was excellent."

I replied, "Oh yes, I almost forgot about the seminar, Plato's cave. Yes, it was interesting, indeed. Did Plato imply that all that we see in this world is illusionary shadows, reflections of another real world?"

Sarah said, "Yes, and we think these shadows are real because we do not know or see any other reality."

I asked, "Which camp would have you joined, Plato or Aristotle? Idealism or realism?"

Sarah said, "Idealism appears good, but I prefer to live in the reality that we have and try to understand it first."

I replied, "But what if reality is just illusions or shadows of the true reality? We would be wasting our time trying to understand it. Like the prisoners in Plato's cave, wasting time to analyze the shadows, they will never understand its true nature without understanding the whole picture."

Sarah asked, "Do you think we will ever be able to understand the whole picture? After all those people in history, scientists, philosophers, priests and theologians, magicians, psychics, doctors, and ordinary men and women. Everyone tried and is still trying to understand, and we are still here in the dark, with no conclusions, not even close. Everybody has a theory, every religion has an idea, and there is no consensus. I think the true reality will never be known, and for sure not in our lifetimes. So, we'd better stick to what appears real in front of us."

"But Sarah," I replied, "With every new scientific discovery, there is hope that things may be revealed. Based on the new understanding, secrets may unravel for the first time. That could happen at any time, with any discovery, with the right brain and the right mind who can put things together correctly. I think we are closer to finding out the truth than we have ever been before."

Sarah said, "I am amazed by your enthusiasm."

I replied, "I am surprised that you prefer materialism."

Sarah, "Why? I am a woman, and I live in this reality! Women always feel reality very deeply. We experience childbirth. What more material reality do you want than that? The material body of the baby physically comes out of our material body, and we feel it completely. It is not an illusion or an idea; it's real flesh and blood."

I replied, "You're right. It definitely should feel that way, but what if pain and our perception of it and the whole thing is also part of the illusion?"

I was surprised that my fellow and potential lover believed the opposite of what I think. We were just like Plato and Aristotle, but in a modern-day scenario, except with different genders in love. It is more difficult that way. History told us that Plato and Aristotle admired and respected each other's ideas until the end. Aristotle held Plato in high esteem and was always citing him in his talks and books, and Plato did the same for him. However, it was only a professional relationship between a student and a teacher. With Sarah and me, it is also that, plus a potential love relationship, at least one that I was hoping would happen.

Could I love Sarah with her opposite opinions? Would I love her less or more because of our differences? Good questions, but I thought it should not have an impact on my love for her. Thoughts, ideas, and beliefs should be different from love; the two concepts are on two different pages. If we were on the same page of love, but different pages of ideas, that would be okay. If I genuinely love her, I shouldn't try to change her thoughts because I also should love them and respect them.

Moreover, it would be selfish for me to change her opinion so that I could love her more. In other words, if I demanded that she change her ideas, so I could love her, that would mean I love myself more than her, or I love my thoughts more than I love her. Therefore, I voted that love should grow strong even with our nearly opposite points of view. It should be even stronger because of the additional elements of respect and admiration, rather than submission and passivism.

On the other hand, would I risk losing my ideas if I accepted hers? Just like Plato lost his idealism to Aristotle, and the world took a wrong turn until now, until me. This paradigm shift would not have happened if Plato had been more aggressive and assertive and pushed forward with his ideas if he had not been the nice guy. Would history repeat itself with Sarah and me? Would she turn the table on me just as Aristotle did with Plato because I am also a nice guy? Should I defend my ideas like a man and forget about love and not risk the future of humanity again? If I am the modern-day Plato, I do not want Sarah to be the modern-day Aristotle. I would want to change the course of human thoughts towards idealism, and study it better in that respect and prove it to be the right flavor of reality.

But I decided to surrender to the current moment and let it go and see what happens.

We arrived at a small restaurant that had a live band, consisting only of two players, one on a violin and another on an acoustic guitar. We sat down at a table for two, by a window in a far corner of the room. The window had curtains with flowers and pinecones on them. Outside the window, there were flowers at different stages of bloom, all different colors, and the gentle wind blew through them and moved them gently as they appeared to enjoy it. Behind the flowers, there was a small creek with water flowing between some rocks. On the table, a small, faint candle floated on clear water, and a red rose stood in a vase, and the reflections from the candlelight on the water, shed a soft light on Sarah's beautiful lips, eyes, eyelashes, eyebrows, and her dark brown hair.

"What more could I ask for?" I thought. "This is heaven, and it is here now. To hell with Plato and Aristotle; they were ugly anyway. To hell with the whole history of humanity. It is history after all, long gone, who cares about it? To hell with the future of humanity also, who knows what it will be, and who cares about it? To hell my theories and agendas. This moment is the only eternal truth out of all things. We were created just to live a moment like this, and it is what will remain after we vanish from this Earth. The music from this violin and this guitar will remain forever, even after the players vanish. Those players are the instruments for the music, not the other way around. The music is playing itself around their hands, and not the other way around. They exist in this life for that purpose only. They are instruments for this eternal music."

The relationship between the violin and the guitar reminded me of the relationship between particles and waves. The violin's continuous notes represented waves, continuous and fluid. The guitar strings plucking individual notes represented particles present within the waves merging together, composing the harmonious symphony, just like physical matter is also made of discrete particles interchangeable with waves. Everything around us, including our bodies, has a wave and particle duality, just like the notes of the violin and the guitar.

Everything around us was serving this eternal moment, the music, the wine, the rose, the flowers, the candle, the light, the curtains, the window, the creek, the magical water, and the young, gentle waitress. It was magic beyond understanding. How could science explain this moment? How could I explain this feeling scientifically?

The band was playing an old French song titled, "Et Si Tu N'Existais Pas," and without saying a word, I extended my hand to Sarah inviting her to dance. No one else was dancing. I put my arm around her waist, with my hand hugging hers, just like mirror images of each other.

Her hair touched my face, and her fragrance invaded my brain, not only her attractive perfume but also her skin cells, her aroma, her pheromones, and hormone molecules. They went through my nose, found their specific corresponding receptors, and I felt the electric impulses they generated passing from the olfactory bulb through the holes in the base of my skull and directly to the frontal lobe of my brain. They also passed through my trachea, straight to my lungs, to the terminal alveoli, exchanged through its thin membrane into my bloodstream. I inhaled Sarah inside my being like a divine breath, giving me another life. At that moment, she was physically in my blood and my brain. I felt like I had taken all the women inside of me through Sarah. She had been chosen as an ambassador of all women to enter my sacred temple and reunite all males and females as one single being.

I closed my eyes and felt Sarah merging with me. We melted into each other, like two wax figures, melting in the heat of a fire. Like a sugar cube that dissolved in water and both had become a new substance made from a mix of the two. All the characteristics of each substance disappeared in the other, and each one lost its prior characteristics in the new material. In my case, that would include my personality, my ideas, my history, and my future. Sarah and I became one again. We had been one before and had gotten separated during evolution into two halves, and now we were merging to become one again. But this time, it would be forever. I was only a half person and incomplete without her, and finally, we were back to one again, a whole and full one.

I felt Sarah's soft body and gentle curves, complementing my hard body and sharp angles as if our two bodies had needed each other for a very long time. Just like someone who was lost in the desert for a long time and finally found a river. Or someone who always walked barefoot on concrete and walked on the sand of the beach for the first time in his life. I felt that I needed to take Sarah inside of me and to dive inside of her. I felt like invading her DNA and taking her DNA inside of me, especially her mitochondrial DNA. I felt like I needed to kiss her mouth very deeply, to the point of touching her DNA with my tongue. I felt like we needed to mix our DNA in one body, with one soul. A body that is a mix between a male and a female and is neither. A blend of Plato and Aristotle and is neither. Back to the original one cell. It seemed like I'd been looking for this for a long time, for billions of years.

Suddenly, the history of life flashed inside my head. I traced my origin backward to my mother, my mother's mother, and their preceding mother's mother, and so on. I went all the way back to when life started as a single original cell. Life later divided that cell and created a male half and a female half to improve on genetics and favor survival and improvement of the species. Those two halves, however, kept yearning for each other to merge again in a magical process that eliminates time and evolution in a single moment. By joining together, Sarah and I defied time and stuck it to evolution. Millions of years of evolution were erased immediately in a single moment. I saw us as one original cell, like an amoeba, dancing on the floor to this eternal music, before that cell eventually became one with the music, the room, and everything else around us, like a symphony of love.

Even though chemistry played some role in that mix, I felt that electromagnetism had the upper hand. Our electromagnetic fields interacted in a complementary fashion long before we touched each other and attracted us together in a magnetic way. With the looks between our eyes, we shared an unspoken language that made us embrace even before we touched. Chemistry may have played a small role after we touched, but electromagnetism did most of the work, before and after that.

Our hearts use electricity, our brains use electricity, our muscles use electricity, and since electricity and magnetism are one thing, two sides of the same coin, we are electromagnetic beings. We interact with each other and with everything electromagnetically. We can sense things from far away, and we can affect other things from far away as well. All these facts are science, but science never really tried to explain it or explore it scientifically.

I imagined, at the moment of orgasm (hopeful thinking), the electromagnetic energy that had built up gradually and then reached the point of climax. The amplified electromagnetic energy from the two simultaneous orgasms would merge into a single amplified energy field that would vibrate as one and would be felt in the two bodies and the two brains at the same time. Like a duet in a song in concert with each other, or two tuning forks synchronizing their vibrations together. That must be an outstanding feeling. I wondered if I would experience that with Sarah? Could I synchronize my tuning fork with hers? Her electromagnetic field was already tickling mine; I felt it going through my spine, reaching my brain, charging my neurons and shaking my inner core, purifying me, with unknown energy that was yet to be discovered by science. It felt as if we were two electromagnetic beings, like Super Mario and Pauline, interacting via electromagnetic projection inside a game.

I whispered in Sarah's beautiful ear, so close to my lips, "Where have you been? I have been waiting for you for such a long time."

"Since when?" asked Sarah.

"Since the beginning of life, even before." I said, "Since first light appeared in our universe, even before, since all the forces of nature were just one force, one wave. Before evolution and Darwin."

Sarah asked, "Am I that old? Are you?"

I said, "No, not you, your idea, your beauty, your female-ness, we were separated before, and now we have found each other again after millions and millions of years."

"Was that in a past life?" Sarah asked.

"No," I said. "It's the same life, not our own lives but the history of life in the universe. We are just two rep-resentatives of life in general. Two ambassadors, two spokespersons for life."

Sarah said, "Professor!"

I continued to whisper, "Not anymore, I was a professor, but now I am a new student, with a new Ph.D. thesis to work on."

"And what is the thesis?" asked Sarah.

"The science of love," I replied.

The music stopped, and I felt descending from outer space like a space shuttle, returning to Earth with the smoke rising from its corners from the heat of the impact.

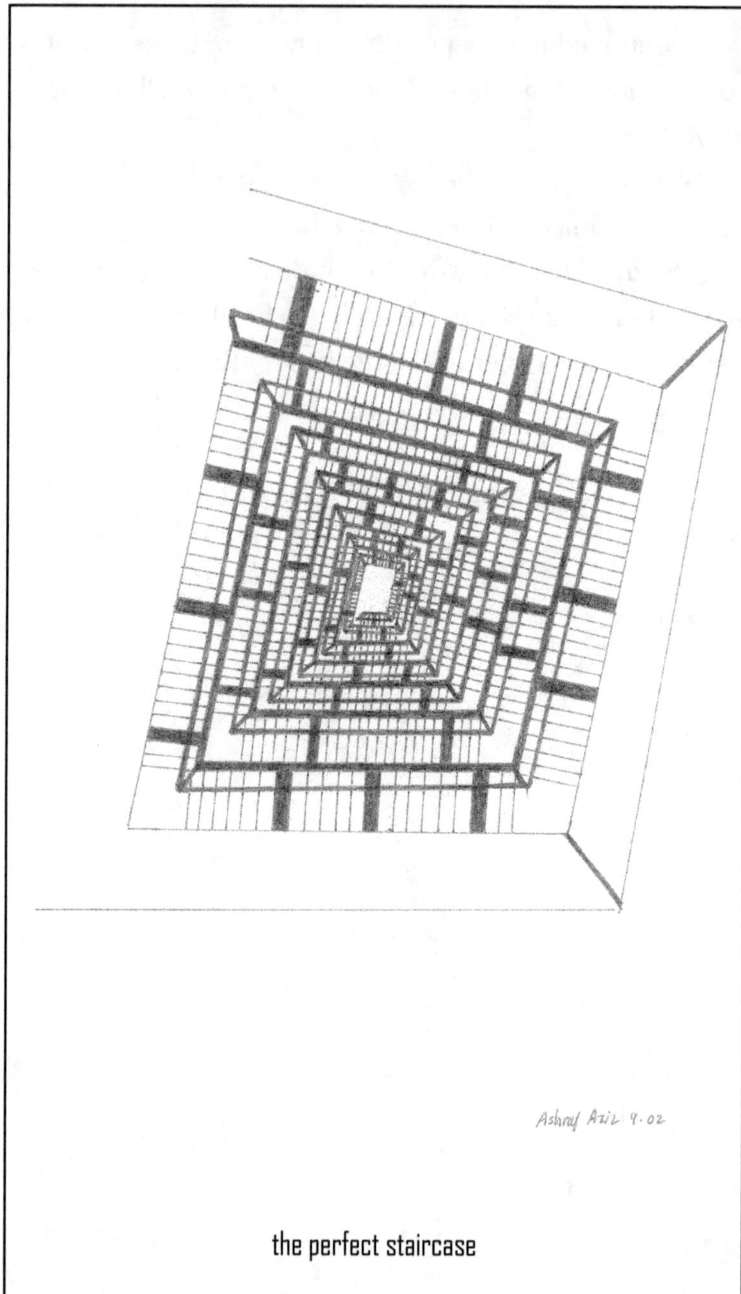

the perfect staircase

CHAPTER 6

Two Different Physics

Later that same week, we were invited to attend a physics seminar titled, "New Science Mysteries," at the university's department of theoretical physics. Sarah had a prior degree in theoretical physics and had a particularly strong background in molecular and quantum physics. She'd started her career trying to be a theoretical physicist but changed gears to neuroscience. She once told me that she thought, neuroscience could probably explain our reality and the nature of our universe better than any other scientific field out there. I was surprised by that statement, but happy, at the same time, that we were both on a similar path since neuroscience is my specialty.

I loved talking to Sarah because she always gave me the scientific perspective from the expert's point of view, sharing new scientific discoveries together and how they could describe and explain our world clearer for us. Every new discovery could be integrated with old knowledge, so we could try to understand reality better based on the latest findings.

"But lately," Sarah said, "Everything is confusing, and reality is becoming murky and much more mysterious based on the new findings."

Sarah always talked about the latest discoveries in science and how interesting and how strange and mind-boggling they were. "It's like we need a new physics to explain the world," she often said.

The speaker started by summarizing the history of science by saying, "Modern science started with the deterministic mentality of Isaac Newton, a clockwork universe, where everything was precisely where it should be, and when it was supposed to go, and everything followed exact, predictable measurements. The universe was like a stage on which everything happened, and time was part of the fixed laws of that stage. About two and a half centuries later, Einstein changed a bit of the reality of the universe and its physics, but he still argued for a determined fixed reality universe even though he radically changed physics altogether. After Einstein, Space and time became one entity, that could be curved and twisted. General relativity had a new description of space-time, and gravity was explained as the bending of the fabric of space-time by heavy objects, like a bowling ball placed on a trampoline, curving it underneath — a new, more precise and accurate way to explain reality. Later, quantum mechanics crept on while Einstein was still alive, changing everything around him and us as if it is describing a different reality, a different world. An undetermined reality based on chances and probabilities. A new uncertain reality."

During the lecture, I realized that there were radical differences between the two types of physics, Newtonian physics, and relativity, on the one hand, and quantum physics on the other. As if they are describing two different reality systems, two different worlds, and the two would never meet because they were both correct but describing two separate things. Scientists struggled and are still struggling to combine the two physics, without realizing that there were two different realities, and each reality has its own different physics. If scientists realized that fact, their lives would become much easier.

As the lecturer was elaborating, I continued to imagine, if we think of our reality as a simulation, like a computer game, like Super Mario, for example, then, Newtonian physics could be describing the world inside the computer game, and quantum physics is describing the physics beyond the computer game, which is propagated through the program. Gravity, for example, exists only in the computer game's reality, as it's part of the game code needed for objects to move and function well inside the game, but it has no existence outside the game. In that case, scientists may never find quantum gravity, as there is no such thing. Gravity is part of the rules of the game program, part of the program code since it is needed for everything to move and fall inside the game and has no existence outside of it.

Newtonian mechanics describes best the physical reality inside of the game, the reality that our brain sees and perceives inside the game program, which is the world around Super Mario, the world that Super Mario sees and feels with his brain inside the program. Everything seems to be deterministic and real. Quantum mechanics, on the other hand, describes the reality beyond the program, which permeates inside and around the boundaries of the program, just like describing the relation between the Wi-Fi and the computer. Quantum mechanics describes the pre-material physics, with its weirdness, like superposition and entanglement, in a similar way that Wi-Fi waves carry information to the computer program. Similarly, in a hologram reality, quantum physics describes the nature of reality beyond the holographic film, like the laser light that shines through the film and goes through the entire hologram. In other words, it is the pre-projector reality.

Scientists must explain both kinds of physics, based on the two different world realities, rather than try to reconcile them. Also, tracking quantum physics, like the Wi-Fi, could lead us to the true reality beyond the computer program, and we should not find gravity there, since gravity is only a function inside the game, not outside.

The question is, I asked myself; how can we see and detect beyond the computer program? Can we try to photograph the Wi-Fi and track it back to its source? In that case, we would need useful imaging devices that could take photographs of things like Wi-Fi or Bluetooth. We would need excellent computer hackers to try to get to the source of the Wi-Fi, hack its computer, and find out more about its nature. Maybe try to take pictures of the person or the team sitting behind the computer by hacking through the computer camera lens to view in the reverse direction and see what is going on in there.

I continued to imagine Super Mario acquiring an AI, and becoming conscious inside his game, realizing his nature, and becoming determined to reach out beyond his game and try to contact the game players, try to attract their attention to his existence as a valuable conscious being. Soon to recognize that he is trapped inside the game, he cannot exit the game reality to experience the outside physical reality because he does not have a physical body. His fundamental nature is just computer codes, that is following the game rules. He has a shape that is visible only on the screen and nowhere else. He and his life are all based on mathematics. He cannot leave the program with his existing characteristics; he has no possible existence outside of the program. Even if he manages to come out of the program, he will never be able to return to the program to change things there or tell his friend, Luigi, what life is like outside the program. He is just like Plato's prisoners inside the cave.

cosmic black and white fireworks

CHAPTER 7

Too Many Mysteries in Science

During the seminar, several scientific mysteries were discussed, and in my mind, I imagined the corresponding explanation based on the two worlds' realities and the two different physics that describe them. If we think differently, there are clear explanations for many of those mysteries.

Here were some examples of the scientific mysteries that the speaker listed in his lengthy talk:

Mystery #1
Physical Matter is empty! Why is there mostly empty space all around us?

When we zoom in or out of our current reality, we see mostly empty space with minimal solid matter present. If we zoom inside our bodies, we find that we are made of molecules and atoms. Zooming in further on atoms, we find that they too are mostly empty space. For example, the hydrogen atom is 99.99999999996 percent empty space. The hydrogen atom consists of an electron and a single proton. To a scale, if the proton is a pea-size thing in the center of a football field, the electron is like a tiny dot, the size of a full stop, like the one at the end of this sentence, hovering around several blocks away from the stadium, and the rest is empty space. However, what is more striking is that the proton is also mostly empty. It is made of three quarks, when combined, only account for about ten percent of the proton's mass, and the rest is, again, empty space.

The nothingness of empty space is not nothing either. There is a constant creation of virtual particles that come in and out of existence all the time.

In the other direction, if we zoom out into outer space, it is also mostly empty; the space between galaxies and clusters of galaxies is mostly empty, and everything is expanding at an accelerated rate, creating even more vacant space.

The other strange phenomenon inside the atom is that electrons are only allowed to exist in specific orbits around the nucleus, and they cannot exist in between those orbitals, just like occupied apartments in a building. Electrons can change orbitals up or down, without traversing the space in between the orbitals. So, they disappear from one orbital and appear in the next orbital without any traces of them in between, as if they are made of digital data bits, zeros and ones, and nothing else. It would be as if I disappeared from the third floor and appeared on the fourth floor of the apartment building simultaneously, without going up the stairs. Nothing in our known reality behaves this way. Even the most solid and compact matter we see around us, like rocks and steel rods are all mostly empty spaces.

Mystery #2
What is dark matter and dark energy?

Another astonishing fact is that everything we see as matter in the universe is only four percent of what exists. The rest is dark matter, around 27 percent, and dark energy, about 69-70 percent, and we still don't know what the nature of either of them is.

Ninety-six percent of the universe is made of matter unknown to us, and the four percent that is known matter is 99.99999999 percent empty. It seems that physical matter is an illusion rather than physical, as there is very little physical stuff. It is like the physical matter in a digital picture or a hologram or a video game. We see the vast universe around us, but it's all like a digital picture frame, and we are also inside that picture and perceiving reality inside the picture. The whole thing is made of pixels, including us. What we see as matter is just the matter inside the image in the digital picture frame, the digital movie, or the hologram, and not the physical matter of the real stuff. It isn't a vast universe after all; it's a picture of a vast universe. That's why matter is just a tiny fraction of what we see. Just like a picture of mountains and the matter is just the matter inside the picture of the mountains and not the matter of the mountains themselves. The matter in the digital picture of the mountains weighs nearly nothing, but the physical matter of the real mountains should weigh millions and millions and millions of tons.

Scientists are trying to discover the nature of physical matter in the mountains, but instead, they should try to discover the nature of matter in the digital picture of the mountains. Otherwise, they are wasting their time. Once we imagine that our universe is just a projection or a simulation, everything would make sense all of a sudden. Time also becomes an illusion; it exists only in the brain due to the passing of sequential frames, a phenomenon created by the brain due to memory. Our brain creates the reality of physical matter, space, and time, or space-time, all around us.

I thought to myself for a moment, yes, I always wondered about the vastness of the universe, how massive it is, and how mind-boggling it is, and I couldn't believe this was all real. The vastness of our universe is better explained as an illustration or a digital image, rather than something physically vast. That makes the universe much more economical. The Big Bang must have been the start point of the projection of that simulation, or the initial start of the computer game, or the digital projection, or whatever it is. Since time is an illusion, then, the entire timespan of this simulation could be hours or days. It could be the length of a movie, but it seems like forever for us because we are trapped inside it. We are imprisoned by its vastness, and laws, almost like ants in the kitchen in my apartment in Toronto. They would never know their place in the apartment, in the city, in Canada, on Earth, the solar system, the Milky Way galaxy, or let alone in the universe. They are also prisoners in their space-time frame, just like us.

The number of galaxies in the observable universe has been increasing as our visual technology improves and was recently estimated as two hundred twenty-five billion galaxies, up from the one hundred billion we knew about just twenty-five years before, and it's likely to increase as better and better telescopes are built. Each galaxy contains an average of one hundred billion stars like our Sun. Our larger-than-average Milky Way galaxy has between two hundred and four hundred billion stars, and we are circling one of them. The number of planets in the universe could be ten to the power of twenty-four planets like Earth.

And I was still thinking, as a neuroscientist, all this truth should be existent in our brains somewhere. The brain is the key to discover this reality, and nothing else can. I could not believe that neuroscience could eventually explain the universe better than physics, cosmology, and astronomy and alongside, explain the nature of time. Everything is known in the mind.

Mystery #3
$E = mc^2$ and $E = hv$, then; $hv = mc^2$

Albert Einstein's most famous equation linked matter m, to energy e, as if they are two sides of one coin. The tiny amount of matter that we observe in the universe is exchangeable with energy, a tremendous amount of energy, when mass is multiplied by the speed of light squared c^2. So, the whole universe could have been started by the energy from a clap of two sheets of branes, or maybe, a clap of two hands creating physical matter in between them. The second equation is the Planck's equation, $E = h\nu$, relating the energy of electromagnetic waves E, equals h (Planck's constant), multiplied by v (the frequency of the electromagnetic waves). And the last elegant equation listed above, came from Louis de Broglie in 1924, by combining both equations, $h\nu = mc^2$, linking mass m, to v (the frequency of the electromagnetic waves) multiplied by Planck's constant h, suggesting that all matter has also wave properties at the same time. This concept is known as the de Broglie hypothesis, an example of wave-particle duality. He discovered that every particle of matter with mass and velocity must be associated with a real wave. Simply by substituting mass m, for energy e, in the two equations, Louis de Broglie was able to discover a new nature of matter. Matter also follows wave property just like energy waves, because mass and energy are two faces of the same coin.

Therefore, what holds true for elementary particles, for example, in the double-slit experiment, mentioned later in this chapter, also holds true for larger atoms and matter in general, including us.

The wave-like behavior of matter was confirmed subsequently in many experiments with different elementary particles, like electrons, neutral atoms, and even small molecules.

Pausing here and thinking for a minute, physical matter is 99.99999996 percent empty space, and what is considered the leftover matter is interchangeable with energy and has wave-like properties.

Looking at these facts, it appears that physical matter is just an illusion; it is what our brain sees and perceives, but it only exists inside our brain. It only appears real to us due to our brain's perception of it as real. Physical matter is better explained as if reality is made of pixels, arranged into images that we see as real.

Also, as we go, reality is created in front of us, like a red carpet that is placed in front of us only in our direction and not pre-existing there. Like a movie studio cast scene, where the direction of filming is the only one that's neat and decorated, and the rest is messy until filming goes there. Reality is better explained as a mathematical model, like a program code written in zeros and ones, which are the basic building blocks of our reality. The smallest possible unit of length measurement, the Planck length, and nothing is possibly smaller than that. The Planck length measures 1.6 X 10 to the power of minus 35 meters, or 10 to the minus 20 power smaller than a proton.

The Planck density is the Planck mass divided by the Planck volume, which is approximately 10 to the power of ninety-three grams per one cubic centimeter, which is a huge wobbling number. That's how many Planck's size-objects that can fit in a cubic centimeter of space.

The basis of quantum mechanics is that everything is quantized, and the smallest quanta size is the Planck length, but we do not know what it looks like, or what it is made of, a string, a point-like particle, or a binary code of zeros and ones, or tiny black holes. If the ultimate zoom into our reality reveals the zeros and ones, and if that smallest thing is a string, then it may have two different shapes, a long string, like a 1, and a closed string like a 0, and everything is built from them, like a computer code. It could be physically 0s and 1s made of strings at the Planck length. The big problem is that we will not be able to see those for a while, and even if we eventually develop the technology to see them after hundreds or thousands of years, they will likely trick us and disappear and decide to go out of existence.

It appears that we and our current present reality are in the middle partition of the program code, halfway between the smallest and the largest. If we can zoom in or out of our current position, for example, go back to earlier codes, or go forward to more complicated codes, we could exactly know our past and peek at our future. Theoretically speaking, we can zoom in to see the level of zeros and ones, the smallest units of our universe, and zoom forward to the last codes, the edges of our reality, the edges of our universe. But unfortunately, the program codes are vastly written, and we are stuck in the middle of it, prisoners in space and time within it. The codes were written that way, and we don't know why. We just stumbled on this information as we became smarter, conscious beings inside the program. We discovered our code.

Mystery #4

The variability of time and other things according to Einstein

Einstein proved that time is relative, and could vary, according to position, direction, and speed, and is also personal to everyone. If you speed up in velocity, your time slows down, and you age less than if you are going at a slower speed. If you travel close to the speed of light, your mass becomes much heavier, and your length contracts along the direction of the motion, you become more compact. With high-speed velocity, clocks tick slower until time stops at the speed of light.

In other words, our daily observations are very much stable, and appear the same and constant to all of us, but once we deviate from the routine, narrow and steady physical state around us, everything changes, such as time, mass, and along with it, also our shape and image, everything changes except for the speed of light.

Like an image broadcasted from a projector on a screen, when you change the angles of projection, the picture gets distorted because it is just an image and not the real thing. Similarly, with relativity, if we play around with some numbers, speed up, for example, we distort the illusionary stuff. The things that came up from our inventions and imagination, things like time, mass, and shape.

This distortion of reality based on relativity in extreme situations, should not happen to real objects but can happen to images, digital projections, holograms, or movies.

Our reality has a very narrow window, a small margin, in which it can exist as we know it. Focus in or out of that margin, and the images become distorted and fuzzy. Our reality is just images then, focused on a narrow surface, like a flat-screen monitor. We exist as digitized images on that thin surface, and if we try to venture outside of it, the images become distorted and blurry. If we manage to venture out of that screen, we would lose our current image and likely lose ourselves in the process.

The speed of light is the only constant in Einstein's equations; everything else is changeable, like time and mass, and hence, shape. The speed of light is the only constant as if everything is made of images, images made from light, and not real stuff.

The light from the cosmic microwave background, or CMB, is still traveling to us from the beginning until now, and we are just seeing that same light now, 13.7 billion years or so after it left the CMB. Time is a function of the internal observer that is us. It is our invention, a measuring stick that we created, like rulers and yardsticks, and is not relevant to an outside observer. So, the lifespan of humanity could be no more than the running time of an average movie, of two- or three hours' duration to an outside observer.

Mystery #5
The Anthropic Principle, Goldilocks Universe

Why was the universe just right for life, and for us eventually, to evolve in it? Just like Goldilocks and the three bears, when the porridge was just right, not too cold and not too hot, similarly, the physical conditions we live in, here on Earth, are remarkably fine-tuned for our existence and development. Any minor changes in the physical laws and life would not have happened the way it did. With small changes, like a slight difference in temperature or the position of the Earth from the Sun, life would not have evolved. If Earth's magnetic field were less or more, the cosmic rays would have destroyed life through a series of genetic mutations. If the Moon weren't there or was not in its exact position, if not for Jupiter and Saturn blocking asteroids and meteors from destroying us. If not for the existence of mountains, exactly where they are and the way they condense the clouds, there would not have been freshwater, and rivers present for life to thrive. And so on for the entire history of life on Earth, for roughly 3.5 billion years, shortly after the formation of Earth, around 4.5 billion years ago. The emergence of life also depended on many similar Goldilocks events that happened in the universe long before life's beginning, like the creation of higher elements, for example, inside massive stars and supernova explosions. The ingredients of life were cooked in the entire universe long before even life began on Earth. Life is a recipe made from the universe.

With that extreme fine-tuning in mind, I doubt that life, as we know it, exists anywhere else in the universe but here. There is no way for life to be present anywhere else with the improbability of events coming together so perfectly, always at the right time and sequence.

With that concept in mind, life, including us, were either intentionally cultured here on Earth, just like E. coli bacteria on a petri dish, planted in the perfect conditions to grow. Or, the other possibility is that our perfect universe is just a projected image on a screen or a computer monitor, where the laws are perfectly set for the projection to occur. The right temperature, the right pressure, the right energy, and the right chemical composition; otherwise, the picture would not have projected correctly. We only exist on the screen, where all these laws come together perfectly, and the image is projecting very well, not too bright and not too dim.

Mystery #6
The universe is probably flat.
In the past, I used to imagine our universe as an air bubble that started from a membrane, and someone was blowing it up like the air bubbles that children blow every day in the park. Dark energy would be explained as the positive energy force of that someone blowing. It's estimated that dark energy is responsible for seventy-five percent of the energy in our universe and is causing the universe to expand. Scientists have shown that the expansion fluctuates in the history of the universe; sometimes it slows down, and sometimes it speeds up, and that is because whoever is blowing is taking a deep breath in between the blowing.

Dark matter would be water and carbon dioxide, from his breath, and galaxies and stars would be like chunks of his saliva or rotating candy within the air bubble. If the air bubble burst open, our universe would scatter and disappear. For us, I imagined that we are living in that universe, while it is being blown up, and it could explode at any moment.

Another time, I imagined the universe as a growing watermelon. Dark energy would be the energy produced by the negative force inside the watermelon, that is exerted by the watermelon's wall as it grows and expands. Galaxies would be the seeds inside it, and dark matter would be the red flesh of the watermelon. We only see the seeds (galaxies) inside, and we have not discovered what the red stuff is made of yet, and we call it dark matter. The universe is expanding as the watermelon grows bigger and the seeds are moving away from each other, just like Hubble discovered. When the watermelon stops growing, our universe will stop expanding, and then, we know that it is ripe and is ready to be eaten. Someday, someone will cut it open, eat it, and throw away the seeds. We are practically parasites living inside one of the seeds.

On another occasion, I imagined the universe like fireworks. If we look at the universe from outside and record it with a very high-speed video camera, we can see that stars are born, shine for a while (a few billion years), and finally fade away into darkness. To an outside observer, someone with a different space-time scale, the universe could be observed like one of the 4th of July fireworks. With that scale of space and time, we would be mostly invisible. Our size and time scales are so small and brief that it wouldn't be noticed by that observer. The time of our whole human existence is so brief, just like a very short movie scene that disappears if you fast forward the tape or CD. In that model, the universe would end up with a void after all the fireworks scatter and burn.

The speaker was describing that scientists discovered that the universe is largely geometrically flat and is expanding just like a sheet of paper, stretching in all directions, but remaining a flat sheet. This flatness is a remarkable and unexpected feature of the universe, which is very hard for us to imagine.

Results from the BOOMERanG experiment (Balloon Observations Of Millimetric Extragalactic Radiation ANd Geophysics) along with other experimental data from other independent sources suggested that the universe is largely flat. The BOOMERanG measured an angle between two points on the cosmic microwave background (CMB) as observed during three, high-altitude balloon flights over the North and South Poles. Following simple Euclidean vs. curved geometry principals, scientist concluded that our universe is geometrically flat.

But we see the universe as a 3D structure around us, as a sphere with us inside it while it is expanding. Again, our magical brain comes to the rescue, and it doesn't look flat for us. Reality is translated by our brains for us to see everything the way it is, but that reality only exists inside the brain, not outside.

Our universe is geometrically flat, just like a curtain, a flat-screen, or a flat digital computer monitor, or in case of the air bubble universe described above, now it is like a flat air bubble membrane, and we are stuck on its surface while it is being stretched in all directions. That flat universe, with us in it, resembles pixelated projections on a flat-screen. Our morphology and all the shapes we see inside our universe are all images displayed on a flat-screen, and our brains see and perceive us, and everything around us, as actual reality since we live inside that projection.

Mystery # 7
The Holographic Principle

Black holes are present everywhere in the universe, at least one in every galaxy. Our Milky Way galaxy has an enormous one in the middle of it. These bizarre galactic beings have unique physics of their own that pushes the limits of imagination. Their internal gravity is so strong that nothing can escape from it, including light. That's why they appear black. When objects fall into a black hole, like me, you, or a giant star, the 3D data of the information of those fallen objects can be encoded on a 2D flat surface. All the information needed to describe the 3D objects is present fully intact on a 2 D surface. The maximal entropy is best explained with the radius squared, not cubed as might be expected. The informational content of all the objects that have fallen into the black hole might be entirely contained in surface 2D fluctuations at the event horizon and can be seen that way by an outside observer. If two people are traveling in space, and one of them happens to fall into a black hole, his friend will see him as a flat image inside the event horizon, like a flat cartoonish image, not as a 3D structure. But the fallen person would continue to see himself the same as his usual 3D version, to which he's accustomed. This is what scientists call, "The Holographic Principle".

In a hologram, there is a 2D film or a screen that has all the detailed information of objects engrained on it. When light, like scattered laser beams shines through the film, it projects the images of those objects as 3D images in front of it, best in a dark space. But in case of black holes, it is the reverse; the hologram 3D images condense into the 2D flat surface. A black hole is like a hologram in a reverse mode.

Again, with extreme physical strain, like inside the intense gravity of a black hole, matter distorts. The 3D objects revert to their original nature of 2D, and with even more stress and strain, that matter would return to its original unified waveform, like the unified plasma, seen in the Bose-Einstein condensate, (described later in this chapter), and even with more extreme physics, back to its original information and digital nature.

In that sense, could black holes be an information outlet from our universe to the reality beyond the universe, like exit points for information, possibly for a hard drive, or a computer processor, or a digital storage device?

What if our universe is a form of a digitized holographic projection? That would be more economically sensible than a vast universe full of stuff. If that is the case, we need to know that fact to be able to explain the true nature of our universe, based on a simulation projection, rather than a physical existence of matter. Otherwise, our equations are wrong, and they will not lead us anywhere meaningful.

Mystery # 8
The Double-Slit Experiment, the Delayed Choice Quantum Eraser Experiment, and the observation problem

In its original version, in 1803, the double-slit experiment proved that light is a wave. When light passes through a barrier with two slits, we see wave interference patterns, a panel of several striped dark and white lines. Einstein proved that light is also made of particles, called photons. A later version of the double-slit experiment tested single particles. Sending particles through a double-slit apparatus one at a time. Astonishingly, an interference pattern also emerged when these particles were allowed to build up one by one at a time, indicating that the single photon or electron, must have passed through both slits at the same time and interfered with itself. This demonstrates the wave-particle duality, which states that all matter, including us, exhibits both wave and particle properties. This phenomenon has been shown to occur with photons, electrons, atoms, and even some molecules. All seen as waves, until we try to observe it, for example setting up a detector or a camera to detect which slit the photon or the electron passed through, we get a particle pattern with just two white lines corresponding to the two slits. Remove the observation or the detector, and you get a wave pattern again. It's as if the photon or the electron knows that it is being watched. This is what scientists called the observation problem, and it continues to baffle everyone until this day, offering no clear answer to why the electron should behave differently when being observed. It is like playing peek-a-boo with elementary particles. In the later designed, delayed quantum choice experiment, and even when the observation was made after the electrons departed, the outcome was still the same, indicating that they may have gone back in time and changed the way they started, depending on what you did later. It is always the same when an observation is made seconds, or even weeks later.

It seems that everything around us, including us and the universe, is made up of tiny data bits, like how a digital photo is made of pixels on a computer screen. These fundamental units of space and time would be unbelievably small; a hundred billion, billion times smaller than a proton. And like the quantum behavior of matter and energy, these bits of space-time would behave more like waves than particles. Space-time is made of waves instead of particles. Everything is jittery and never sits still until an observation is made. Just like teenagers having a messy party, but when their parents arrive, everything is neat and tidy, and everything is back to where it is supposed to be.

Many non-scientists and philosophers attribute the observation problem to our consciousness or to a universal consciousness that collapses the wave function whenever it observes anything, but I see it differently. I think of the universe and ourselves as manifestations of a single particle, like one electron in different forms and shapes that only appear to us as material things, matter, or images. The probability sum of the observer and the observed cannot be more than one when interacting together. So, in a world when you are observing the photons going through the double slit, it cannot give you a wave pattern because the probability would be more than one in that case, and that is mathematically impossible. Every probability must add up to a maximum of one and not more. The solution of the observation problem is not due to our conscious mind, not at all; it is due to the mathematical nature of everything equated by the interaction between the half-particle of the photon and the other half-particle which is us. Without observation, there are endless possibilities for positions of the photon, but once we observe it, we interact with the particles, and the sum of the probability interaction becomes 1, not infinity +1. That's why we never observe and see a wave pattern; we will never get infinity +1.

At that time, I also remembered that elementary particles have no identity for themselves. Two electrons, for example, will always have precisely the same charge, mass, and total spin. There's no property of the particle that lets you paint a number on the side of it. All electrons are the same as every other electron, just like Agent Smith in the movie "The Matrix," when there was an infinite number of him fighting and multiplying in any direction at any time as needed, and all of them were the same size and shape, with no identity. Could there be just one electron or one proton in the entire universe, with many copies as needed?

The no-identity role of elementary particles also resembles the digitized nature of everything. Everything is made up of digital zeros and ones, and with that, there is no individual identity for either the zero or one. All zeros are the same, and all ones are the same. Just like the no identity rule for natural numbers, like the number 2, or number 7, for example, all number 2s are the same as any other number 2, and you could write it as a 2, think about it in your head as a 2, or see it as a concept everywhere as a 2.

Mystery # 9
Matter and antimatter, and why is there matter out there rather than antimatter?

Energy produces particles of matter and antimatter at the same time and in similar quantities, but if they get in touch, they annihilate each other back to energy again. For example, a pair of an electron and a positron would puff out of existence with a flash of light. Every day, I review patients' PET scans (Positron Emission Tomography), which takes pictures of this transient interaction when positrons are emitted from radioactive sugar, injected into the patient's veins, and taken in by the rapidly dividing cancer cells. Once the antimatter positrons are emitted, they immediately become annihilated in fractions of a second by their counter-matter electrons, and that interaction produces tiny flashes of light that we detect in the image of the malignant tumor, anywhere in the body.

Antimatter was predicted back in 1928, by Paul Dirac, in his paper describing the quantum theory of electrons. He saw the equations equally correct with positive and negative results, both yielding right outcomes. He predicted the existence of antimatter from the mathematical equations. Later, Carl Anderson discovered the positron in 1932, by studying showers of cosmic particles, in a cloud chamber in Caltech, in California.

Antimatter also could be seen in the universe. In a unique type of star explosion, called a particle pair, when the hot core of a very massive star, (150-300 solar mass) gives rise to pairs of matter and antimatter particles, which cause a premature blast, followed by nothing. Everything disappears as if there was nothing there to start with, no supernova, no black hole, no neutron star, nothing at all left behind, as matter cancels out antimatter within the star. Imagine seeing our Sun do something like that one day, a brief blast followed by a complete dark void of nothing.

The lesson I got from this talk was, if you see your antimatter you somewhere, try your best to avoid him. You do not want to shake his hand at any cost.

The question is; why was matter created with antimatter? Are both just mathematical concepts? Just like Paul Dirac predicted from the equations long before the discovery of antimatter. Which is the real thing, the equations, or the physical matter?

And the other question is; Why is there matter rather than antimatter? When it should have been nothing.

Scientists speculate that matter exists because of a slight shift in the tendency of B mesons to spend more time in matter mode more than antimatter mode. B mesons shift between matter and antimatter state, but they spend about 50.05 percent of their time in matter state, and 49.95 percent in antimatter state, and matter exists because of that 0.05 percent advantage. Therefore, matter exists due to a borrowed, slight time advantage, and if it is given enough time, it will be erased, or given back to the bank. The other speculative theory of why there is matter, rather than antimatter, comes from a possible disparity between matter neutrinos and their antimatter neutrinos counterparts. Scientists are still trying to figure out the reason why matter exists.

Surprisingly, antimatter particles like the positron, for example, goes backward in time. These are real, existing particles that we use every day in our PET scan machine, and they do go backward in time as part of their typical properties. We are made of stuff that is entirely borrowed, borrowed mass, borrowed energy, and likely borrowed time.

The third question is: what if antimatter would have prevailed? What kind of world would that have been? Imagine a world made of antimatter: all negative stuff, evil, ugly, and bad. Maybe our world was the net product after the forces of good (matter) and evil (antimatter) fought, and the forces of matter won and allowed our existence. But the forces of evil antimatter are still watching and ready to take on any lost matter out there. It was a very marginal victory though, just by .05 percent.

In summary physical matter, is mostly empty, is equal to energy, has wave-like properties, and finally, has a strong natural enemy called antimatter that erases it whenever they get together, just as the negative cancels out the positive in simple mathematical equations. The only difference is that, in physical reality, the event happens with a flash of light that can be photographed. Whenever I encounter an equation where positives and negatives cancel each other out, instead of crossing it with a diagonal line, I saw a flash of light in my mind too.

Mystery # 10
Quantum entanglement; Married particles, not necessarily in love
When two particles are created together or interact, entanglement happens between them. The two particles become intimately linked to each other, even if separated by a vast distance, like many light-years away of space. Any change induced in one will affect the other instantaneously but in the opposite direction.

If one particle says, "up," the other particle instantly says, "down," if one says, "left," the other automatically will say, "right," and in the opposite spin. Just like a married couple, it's not necessarily love; it's entanglement. If it were love, they would have pointed in the same direction, if one said, "up," the other particle would also say, "up," with it. It's not similarity that matters; it's complete complementarity, just like a perfect marriage should be. With nothing in common whatsoever, but able to survive, because it covers every possible aspect of life.

The two particles are actually one, and when they separate, they still behave like one. The addition of the two will equal the one, and the distance between them means nothing to them. The distance only exists in our illusionary universe and is not actually there. The fate of the two particles was written together. They were born together, connected forever, but in opposite directions during their existence, and they will eventually die and vanish together. They are part of a whole system, two halves forming a full one together.

Entanglement was first mentioned in the 1920s, and in the 1930s, it was not swallowed easily by Einstein, as he never believed in it. But later, in the sixties, physicist John Bell proposed tests and experiments that could prove it. Those experiments were done in the late eighties and nineties and indeed confirmed the phenomenon right. Entanglement was demonstrated experimentally with photons, neutrinos, electrons, molecules the size of buckyballs, and even small diamonds.

Entanglement means that those particles are not individual particles but are part of a whole quantum system that is considered an inseparable whole. In entanglement, one constituent cannot be fully described without considering the other(s). The state of a composite system is always expressible as a sum of the products of states of its local constituents.

Is it possible that there are stages or levels of entanglement? Small systems involve two photons, but larger systems can include protons, atoms, balls, people, populations, societies, or the entire universe?

The universe would be a whole, inseparable system, with everything in it is entangled and connected to each other. In that case, we all should add up to one, a whole one; whatever is done in one place affects everyone in another place or time — all in one and one in all.

Mystery # 11
The absolute zero and the Bose-Einstein condensate

Bose-Einstein condensate (BEC) is what happens to a dilute gas when it is made very cold, near absolute zero, close to 0 K (or −273° C, or −459.67 °F). A new kind of matter forms, called Bose-Einstein condensate. Similar to plasma, it has extremely low density and zero viscosity, becomes superfluid, and superconductive, and behaves very different from ordinary matter. It flows upwards against gravity, and seeps out of containers, just like waves. The atoms in the BEC are all exactly the same and are all in the same quantum state. Instead of atoms usually bouncing around, each randomly in different directions, in the BEC, they all bounce together in the same way, forming something called a giant matter-wave. The atoms lose their identity and their interests, and all become one giant matter-wave. Predicted in the 1920s, and finally observed in the 90s, its discovery proved a new state of matter that was never thought of before.

No one knows yet what would happen at an absolute zero temperature; likely there would be no BEC, no plasma, but only energy waves. This is again an example that the stuff that we are made of, has a very narrow range of existence, only around the preset physical standards, and when shifted out of these standards, as with extreme cooling, matter disappears out of existence and becomes energy waves again. Imagine, if we had the technology to cool all the people on Earth near absolute zero, we would all melt into plasma, and become synchronized atoms moving altogether and in the same direction, like waves. Just like cheering spectators in a stadium doing the wave with no identity and no selfishness.

Mystery # 12
The Higgs boson, a.k.a. the God particle

Finally, by discovering the Higgs boson, forty years after it was predicted by Mr. Peter Higgs, the finishing touches were made on the standard model of particle physics. It had to be discovered; otherwise, the whole theory would have been wrong or incomplete. The Higgs particle is associated with its field, which is like an invisible force known as the Higgs field. It is this field that gives mass to all the other fundamental particles; otherwise, they would be massless, like photons of light. Just like different sorts of fish, with different shapes and sizes, move differently in water based on their physical properties; also, different elementary particles move through the Higgs field differently based on their features and properties like massless fishes. Particles have no mass but have other properties of shape, size, spin, and charge, and by moving through the Higgs, they get their mass. Otherwise, they are massless. Again, just like images of something else and not the real thing. We are essentially made of massless particles that borrow their mass by moving through the Higgs energy field, just like a beam of light going through a medium like a plasma screen or an LCD screen and giving rise to a particular shape and morphology and a sensation of a mass with it.

Physical matter, as outlined before, is present in minuscule amounts, is exchangeable with a lot of energy, has wave property, has an antimatter enemy, and has no actual mass of their own. They get their mass as they move through the Higgs field. Physical matter is losing more and more ground every time I think about it.

Madam N.S. and Another Case of Sporadic Fatal Insomnia (sFI)

Late one afternoon in my office, I received a call from my longtime colleague and co-researcher, Dr. Giovani, from Milan University in Italy. He wanted to discuss with me a challenging case of a patient that he was taking care of in the hospital. He summarized the case to me in his Italian accent. "This patient was admitted to Milan University Hospital, about six weeks ago, with deteriorating neurological functions. Madam N.S. (which also stands for never slept) was a thirty-two-year-old woman who had an eighteen-month history of progressive neurological symptoms with attention deficits and progressive memory loss. She demonstrated bizarre behavior, like talking incoherently to herself. The patient's sleep pattern progressively deteriorated throughout her illness. Some nights, the patient did not sleep. On other nights when she did appear to be sleeping, her sleep was intermittent and very superficial. After she progressed, she would go two to three days without sleep. Medications were not helpful to put her to sleep, including narcotics, barbiturates, or benzodiazepines."

Dr. Giovani explained that her sleep studies showed that she was able to have stage one and stage two sleep and go back to wakefulness. She was unable to go to deep sleep, stage three, four, or REM sleep. Later, Madam N.S. died due to her severe deconditioning and loss of function. Her family refused life support due to her very poor quality of life. Postmortem examination showed severe thalamic neuronal loss due to the accumulation of abnormal proteins, called prions.

Dr. Giovani said that they had a family in Milan who had what is called Familial Fatal Insomnia, or FFI, and he initially suspected that the patient might have this disease, but she did not have that family history. He sequenced her genetics and found no mutation in the known gene for FFI, which is codon 129 in the PRNP gene, but he found a polymorphism that can predispose to abnormal prion protein production. PRNP is the human gene encoding for the major prion protein, but scientists still don't know its function in the brain. The abnormal prions are oddly shaped, crooked proteins, and they tend to convert other healthy proteins to become similarly crooked and misfolded like them by contact, just like a drug dealer who is always looking for new victims to turn into addicts. These crooked proteins, lots of them, eventually deposit and clutter in the brain and cause brain damage. In the case of Madam N.S., those proteins completely damaged the neuronal nuclei in the thalamus that are responsible for deep sleep, that is, stage three, four, and REM sleep.

Initially, Dr. Giovani did not know that there were cases of sporadic fatal insomnia, and I didn't know either, but we both found similar case reports in the medical literature.

I apologized to Dr. Giovani that I couldn't be of much help to him. On the contrary, I thanked him for letting me know about this unfortunate but rare interesting case.

Reboot Me While I'm Sleeping

After my conversation with Dr. Giovani, I went to our sleep research lab, pulled one of our senior research fellows, and started asking him questions. This was the easiest way to review the neurophysiology of sleep in detail, instead of going to the textbooks. I loved working in the university with all this information at my fingertips. I had easy access, not necessarily in the library, but inside the brains of faculty, fellows, and students around me. All I had to do was ask questions and listen.

As the fellow was explaining, I translated the information to fit it in my theory, as I always did, without him realizing it.

I went over the stages of sleep and the sleep cycles with him, stages 1, 2 and 3, and 4, then back to stage 2, followed by REM sleep, and then the cycles repeat four to five times during the night.

Each stage has its characteristic EEG waves.

Stages 1 and 2 are like an introduction to sleep, let's say sleep 101, a slow transition from wakefulness. The brain waves slow down further as we go from stage 1 to stage 2.

Then the real sleep comes by, the real coma, with stages 3 and 4, which have the slowest waves called "delta waves." These are also known as synchronized sleep waves, as if many areas in the brain are pulsating at the same time, like a heart or a symphony played in a vast orchestra of one hundred billion musicians.

Stages 3 and 4, are followed by going back up to stages 1-2, light sleep again, then periods of rapid eye movement (REM) sleep, so-called because our eyes move rapidly under the eyelids as if we are awake and seeing things all around us and must look right and left, up and down. During REM sleep, the brain waves mimic those of full awakening waves. Our muscular system becomes paralyzed, just as if we were under anesthesia, so we cannot act out our dreams.

I asked the research fellow to give me the most amazing fun facts about sleep that he'd found during his research.

He replied, "There are so many. I'm not sure what's of interest to you."

I said, "Just amuse me with your most interesting facts and findings."

"Here are some of the facts that amaze me every time I think about them," he said. "We sleep almost one-third of our lives, so for twenty to thirty years, if we live long enough, we are basically in a coma, and we are paralyzed for a good portion of that time, like ten years combined.

"Wow," I said, "I never thought of it that way." Something clicked in my head immediately, "That is very weird and suspicious; it smells like a conspiracy." I thought. "Someone or something must be behind that fact. Thirty years of coma, ten of them in paralysis? That is a lot of coma and paralysis during our lifetime."

The researcher continued to explain, "Babies and infants sleep eighty percent of their time with a very good portion of that in stages 3, 4, and REM sleep. That's when we see them smiling and cute or crying for no reason. As we age, our sleep decreases gradually, primarily stage 3 and 4 and REM, to almost nothing. For example, a ninety-year-old will have practically no deep and REM sleep."

"Growth," he said, "Happens during sleep as hormones, including growth hormones, are secreted."

He explained that sleep happens in almost all organisms, described in as low species like jellyfish and starfishes. "In fact," he said, "Sleep research is mainly done with fruit flies because they are easy to study, and their lifespan is short so that neuroscientists can see quick results." Researchers discovered that many animal species also have REM sleep and dream, and they like to take siestas in the afternoon, as people in Spain. Birds can sleep while flying, and aquatic mammals can sleep floating on water, using half of their brains to keep going while the other half sleeps. Many animals can sleep with one eye or two eyes open for protection and camouflage.

"Many novels and other works of art, such as drawings, paintings, poems, and music compositions, originated during sleep or from dreams, according to their authors," he said. "Also, many scientific discoveries and inventions were made during dreams. The most famous of all scientists was Thomas Edison, who used sleep and dreams intentionally to find answers and solutions for his many discoveries. He used to take naps, with his arms unsupported, so when he falls asleep, his arms drop and wake him up, and voila, there it is, and the answers are there. Among his many discoveries, he also discovered the potential power of dreams to discover new inventions, (double discovery or discovering the source). Another example is the famous Russian scientist, Dmitri Mendeleyev, who discovered the structure of the periodic table of elements after it came to him in a dream. After he was struggling to solve it for three days and three nights straight, he fell asleep on his desk, and when he woke up, he wrote down what had come to him while sleeping, the periodic table of the elements. As if during sleep and while we dream, we tap into an endless source of knowledge, like an information library and unlimited inspiration."

"We have to sleep to stay alive. We can't stop sleeping and continue to live." He stated this very clearly. "If we get sleep deprived for a few days." he added, "Two to three weeks at the most. The maximum in research was eleven days, and we must make it up, particularly deep sleep and REM sleep. According to the experiments, the deep sleep and REM sleep we miss must be exactly compensated for later, at the expense of light sleep, stages 1 and 2, and wake up time". I thought about the implications of this information for a few minutes and said "There must be something fundamental happening there, something essential to our survival, almost like rebooting the computer every night or getting Windows updates during the night; without them, the computer will collapse or malfunction and stop working. If important downloads are missed temporarily, they still must be downloaded later, and it would take the same amount of time to download those updates that were missed before."

He replied in a kind of confused voice, not understanding clearly what I was saying, "Well, yes, something like that." and then he continued to elaborate, "REM sleep and dreams are both known to happen in all mammals and other vertebrates, recently being demonstrated in experimental lab mice."

I wondered why it is so. Why would a frog, a chicken, or a cat dream? And what do they dream about? Sleep and dreams are part of the life program then, and they are deeply ingrained throughout most species. They must have a significant role in our function, survival, and evolution. It would be fascinating to tap into the dreams of animals and figure it out. Maybe someday we would be able to record those dreams and project them like movies.

The researcher continued to say, "Historically, in many cultures, dreams were utilized to predict the future, see faraway events, or interpret known facts and understand if they were good or bad for them. Many ordinary people also described similar experiences. They dream about something as it was happening in another place, far away from them, or they dream of an event before it happens."

I told him, "But that is of course, very hard to measure objectively."

He said, "Yes, indeed, that's why it is all dismissed by scientists."

I said, "I had similar experiences like that before."

He replied, "I think everyone has, at some point, especially when it comes to major events in their lives."

I said, "Please continue; it is fascinating."

He went on further, "Time is very hard to measure during sleep. We could experience a minute in a dream when it was actually hours or spend hours and think it was just minutes. Time perception is totally different during sleep and dreams."

I said, "So in summary, we do not know what is really going on during sleep, especially REM sleep. Where do we go? Or who updates or reboots our program for us to function correctly? Is it a back-and-forth data exchange, like collecting data from a robot and giving it instructions? What kind of program is it? And where is the server? And who is behind it? A team or an individual?"

The researcher appeared very confused after my questions were thrown at him as if a bucket of ice-cold water was poured on him suddenly.

He replied in a sort of robotic manner, "These questions are beyond the scope of my research, we are just trying to understand the basics of sleep physiology."

I replied, "Sure, sure, I understand, but next comes the practical questions; could we discover this reality? What kind of experiments and technology would we need to design to explore it? Sleep is very ubiquitous, something we and everyone do every day, and there is no shortage of it. We could all be subjects for research every night."

I thanked the researcher for his entertaining discussion, went straight to my office, and started thinking.

We need to develop new detectors, or sensors, to photograph what happens during slow-wave sleep and REM sleep or even use a computer hacking team to tap into the source behind the sleep.

Since our waking life and our observable world is likely an illusion, could dreams be the true reason for our existence? Our real job starts there, when we go to bed, we start working. Our hard life during the day is an illusion, and our real function starts during sleep and dreams. We start working hard once we hit the bed and sleep, whether it is an entertainment job, research job, exploration job, or a simulation job.

Since time is also an illusion, that is, our daily waking time, we could be living much longer in our dreams than we think, and our waking time could be very brief. For example, our entire lifetime could be just an hour, and the entire lifetime of the universe could be represented during a movie running time of only two to three hours. The time span of a dream could be the whole lifetime of our existence.

We are living a double life, just like Dr. Jekyll and Mr. Hyde, one is true life during sleep, our real purpose of existence, and another one is the illusionary ordinary life we live every day, and we think it is our only true real life. Our daily reality could be a continuous persistent long dream that we experience when we wake up every morning, except for the fact that it is continuous, like a TV series. When we wake up, we actually, in fact, go to sleep from the true other reality during the night, and when we sleep at night, we actually, in fact, wake up to that other reality, which may be the real true purpose in this life of ours.

To reach the ultimate answers, we need collaboration between neuroscientists, physicists, biologists, computer scientists, including professional computer hackers, pharmacists, anesthesia specialists, hypnosis experts, psychiatrists, and maybe also, mind-readers, mentalists and last but not least, psychotics. A difficult task that needs tremendous effort and resources to be achieved.

The first step is to pinpoint and identify precisely the brain centers that are in control for slow-wave synchronized sleep and REM sleep and stimulate them 100-fold or so. We could use high-frequency deep brain stimulation by implanting electrodes directly in those brain centers.

Secondly, we need to inhibit the conscious brain in deeper levels than usual, to eliminate any conscious interference with the experiment. Besides, we need to stimulate the memory centers in the hippocampus, fifty to sixty-fold, to be able to remember the dreams vividly, and analyze them thoroughly, to see if it is possible to make sense of what they are and what they mean.

Thirdly, we need to follow the synchronized waves from the brain and trace it to a common source. We may need to invent a device that can trace Wi-Fi waves and take pictures of them connecting or going to a power source and maybe trace that power source to a more central power source, and then to the primary source, or the server. We can use the expertise of a professional hacking team to follow the waves, just as if they can follow Bluetooth waves to their source and photograph the source if possible through the computer camera, or, if possible, maybe try to hack and change some of the programs, like corrupt the hardware and see its effects on our world.

Dreams and synchronized wave sleep are windows that allow us to look outside our reality and see the true reality; it is also like access to infinite and endless visions, inspirations, and information. By tapping into this source of knowledge scientifically, I am sure we would be able to discover our missing true reality and be able to solve the nature of our consciousness, especially the hard question of consciousness. Understanding it should bring us closer to the source of our existence than our fake illusionary everyday reality. This illusory reality that is consuming us and acting very well to distract us from knowing and discovering the truth.

What happens during sleep? Where do we go? Do we visit a parallel universe with parallel forms of us in it? Are we subjects in a computer game being played with during sleep? Why do we see what we see in dreams? And why do we see stuff that we have never seen before in our entire life? Are we subjects of entertainment or research and we are performing our real functions in sleep? Are we born to sleep? Is that why reproduction is programmed into life, including our system, basically to bring more and more sleeping babies? The life program unconsciously, implanted in us and all plants and animals, the urge to reproduce and deliver more efficient and adaptable young forms of ourselves.

Is the motivation to bring more and more effective sleepers? Babies sleep much more efficiently than older people, and it is also true for baby animals.

Is that also why we die? Because we lose efficiency to sleep, especially REM sleep. In other words, as we age, we do not perform our job well, and we become useless in it. A ninety-year-old trying to entertain, perform, do research or exchange information would be practically useless, a waste of time and effort. It would be better to recycle him into a new and more useful member or player.

And now another important question; would we live longer if we figure out a way to increase deep and REM sleep? Would we become more valuable and deserve to live longer if we do that? Would we become significant enough to live longer if we could also improve our memory and sleep better? Important research questions for the future. I think all this research is better to be conducted on humans, not animals, in order to gather and document actual experiences and data.

"The day science begins to study non-physical phenomena; it will make more progress in one decade
than in all the previous centuries of its existence."

Nicola Tesla

Designing the Right Experiments

I quickly realized that the prior proposal was such a huge task, and it would require a tremendous effort in collaboration, research grants, and labor, that my entire life may not be long enough to achieve. Also, I may not find enough funds and interested people to carry on a project like that. It seems to be purely based on my theories, ideas, and goals. I decided to proceed with the initial steps with Sarah and see first what kind of results we get.

The first step is easy; Ask the neuroscience research fellows for detailed information about the brain centers involved in sleep.

The second step is to seek help from pharmacists and anesthesia to develop the right drugs for the experiment. Also, by using laser combined with electrical/magnetic stimulation, such as transcranial magnetic stimulation (TMS) to target the corresponding brain centers involved. The combination of laser with TMS is important to deliver a pinpoint stimulation guided by the laser and delivering the stimulating power of TMS directly to the involved center. Some of the delivery access would be better aimed through the mouth directly to the Medulla, and the brain stem directly behind it.

Once we have the right brain centers located and identified, find the right drugs, and tools, I will ask Sarah to inject me with those drugs, and I will record the findings when I wake up. It is that simple. I need to ask Sarah for her approval to participate. She knows my mission, but now it is on a different level of the game. It is getting serious now.

First, I identified those brain centers of interest within the brain that are responsible for stages 3 and 4 sleep and REM sleep.

Briefly described by one of the fellows, "The initial sleep trigger happens with the secretion of melatonin from the pineal gland. In birds and amphibians, where the skull is transparent, the pineal gland can sense the absence of external light and the arrival of night, and the need to sleep. That triggers the secretion of melatonin. But in humans, like us, due to our thick skulls, light cannot go through. Instead, there is another circuit from the back of our retinas that travels to the suprachiasmatic nucleus to the hypothalamus and back to the same pineal gland, and that triggers the secretion of melatonin. Melatonin has been isolated and used as an oral medication to induce sleep, and in research and pharmaceutical laboratories, it's also available as an intravenous drug. Also, similar effects are achieved with Propofol and Thiopental, which are used to induce coma under anesthesia."

I preferred to use intravenous melatonin because it is a naturally secreted substance in the brain. The intravenous form has immediate and more powerful effects. Intravenous melatonin has not been studied in humans, but I'm willing to give it a try on myself. We must obtain some of it from our research lab, or should I say, "Borrow some?"

The centers involved in REM sleep are situated in what is called the ventral medulla. That's why REM sleep is very ubiquitous in nature; it's located in a very primitive part of the brain, that we share with nearly all existing animals, like the fruit fly, for example. Those neurons induce REM sleep using GABA (gamma-aminobutyric acid), the main inhibitory neuro-chemical used in the brain. In experimental rats, it was possible to induce REM sleep rapidly and more frequently when laser beams stimulated this area. It would be possible to try this on myself under a functional brain MRI scanner, where that center can be precisely located and stimulated with a laser beam augmented by TMS. As a brain surgeon, I could also plan for insertion of a small, implantable, high-frequency deep brain stimulation electrode that can be manipulated from the surface wirelessly. This technique has been done in research before for Parkinson's disease and is best if done directly under EEG (electroencephalogram) monitor, to correlate with the right brain waves, and EMG (electromyography), to continuously monitor muscular activity during this process. During sleep, our muscles should be totally paralyzed so that we don't act out our dreams, and that paralysis is a direct indication that we have entered the REM sleep territory.

The reticular formation, a network of nerve pathways, carries signals up and down the brain stem and to the brain. Its function is to inhibit the rest of the brain during sleep or to stimulate it for us to wake up. If these fibers get damaged, a person may not be able to wake up and may stay in a permanent coma state, as once happened in research experiments using cats. The cat never woke up.

Memories from dreams are hidden away from the hippocampus (the memory center of the brain), they physically do not reach that center. That's why we forget our dreams immediately unless we catch them within a few seconds after waking up. It's possible to stimulate the hippocampus during REM and slow-wave sleep, using laser beams, so that the sleeping person can remember his or her dreams vividly, for us to examine in full detail. Imagine remembering dreams as good as we remember our everyday events, recalling every detail from beginning to end as if we were walking through the dream as we walk through a regular day. It would be a fascinating experience and is theoretically possible experimentally.

The ventrolateral preoptic nucleus, or the VLPN, of the hypothalamus, is also involved in switching between sleep and wakefulness, but it is located deep inside the brain and is difficult to manipulate. Most of the manipulation in that area induces wakefulness. In my research, I would try to avoid that area altogether.

In brief, I'd have to borrow the IV melatonin, the laser beam apparatus, the TMS coil, and the EEG and EMG machines and bring everything, every night, to the MRI suite. That would be a lot of borrowing but is doable.

I first tried summarizing the trial procedure in my head:

First; inject the IV melatonin into the subject; for example, myself, via an intravenous cannula, wait for 10 -15 minutes until I pass through light-wave sleep and get into slow-wave sleep and REM sleep.

Secondly; stimulate the ventral medulla through the mouth with the laser beam, combined with TMS intermittently every 10 -15 minutes, and use the high-frequency deep brain stimulation to do the same thing but to a deeper level. Furthermore, precise and direct stimulation, via injecting neurotransmitters directly in those centers using a tiny implanted port catheter, inserted by a neurosurgeon. This technique will induce deeper and more frequent sleep.

During this stimulatory process, I would need to apply a steel traction face mask to prevent movements during the stimulation, and hence, avoid stimulating the wrong brain centers, which could result in disastrous or fatal adverse events.

Thirdly; inhibit the reticular formation, also through the mouth, to inhibit the rest of the brain more deeply during the dreams, to minimize any interference, and induce more profound paralysis.

Fourthly; stimulate the hippocampus during periods of deep sleep and REM, to remember the dreams vividly and record them in our memories.

I went on imagining the experiment in my head. At the start of the experiment, Sarah would inject me with IV melatonin and monitor the EEG, EMG, and my vitals. She will also determine when it is safe to induce REM sleep and wake me up with stimulation of the reticular formation, as needed, in case of emergency.

Besides Sarah's critical role in this experiment, I would need two more people, at least. One, from the physics department who would try to photograph the slow sleep waves and trace them to a source. And another expert, a computer hacker who would try to hack reality, trace the information back into the source computer or server, to the person or the team behind reality. Or, at least try to corrupt some of the programs and see what effects this interruption would have on our reality experience.

I was very excited to put together the details of the experiment finally in my head. Next, I had to discuss all of it with Sarah and come up with a convincing scenario to get the other two people to join us to start conducting the experiment.

I decided to apply for a research grant from the NIH to study the relationship between the total amount of induced deep sleep and REM sleep duration and longevity in organisms, such as lab mice, or fruit flies. My hypothesis was, "Increasing deep sleep and REM sleep can prolong life span in fruit flies." My real intention was to do these studies on human subjects, mostly myself for now.

This animal research project would allow me to legally use the research equipment of the university, like the Functional MRI scan and the PET scan and get access to all the facilities without suspicion.

I immediately discussed those details with Sarah, and to my astonishment, she didn't seem at all surprised when I opened the discussion, instead, she was as excited as me to give it a shot, but only on one condition. She said, "I want to alternate being the subject of the experiment with you; this will allow me to live the experience and put my independent thoughts and perspective on it."

I was shocked and afraid at the same time. I replied, "What if something bad happens to you? I will never forgive myself."

Sarah replied, "Thanks for your concern, but we are in the same boat together, are we not?"

I said, "Yes, of course, but you are young and beautiful, and life still has lots of things to show you after me."

Sarah looked at me with a worried look and said, "I am not doing this unless you guarantee me that you'll be safe!"

I thought for a moment and looked back at Sarah; I wanted to hug her and tell her that she was the only thing I cared about in this entire life and that I live on the hope that we would be together forever, like one being. Unfortunately, somehow, I could not say any of this to her.

Instead, I replied, "We'll depend on each other's expertise to get through the experiment safely. The only danger is using Propofol or the IV melatonin, and that just requires careful monitoring, that's all. I'll give you a crash course on anesthesia to teach you what to do in case of distress signals. Also, we can be woken up at any time immediately by stimulating the reticular formation or the hypothalamus."

Since I wanted to start the experiment soon, I tried to negotiate with Sarah.

I said, "How about, I will be the subject of the first three to five sessions, and if they turn out safe, you can take a turn once."

Sarah replied, "Three sessions, then it is my turn, and after that, we will alternate every other one."

I said, "Deal, but I will be the only one to have the direct catheter inserted in my brain and the traction iron mask around my face."

Sarah replied, "Yes, of course, I do not want those, I might be crazy, but not to that extent, professor. Besides, the mask will be bad for my skin."

I laughed and said, "Great, all parties have agreed upon the conditions. We need to start as soon as possible; time is running out," I told Sarah. "We'll try to run the experiment every night, as much as it's feasible, especially on weekend nights. With the summer approaching, the university will be mostly empty."

Sarah had several points to add. She asked, "Why not use Propofol instead of IV melatonin since we know exactly how to use it and its pharmacodynamics are well known?"

I replied, "But Propofol will induce a deeper state of coma, and we may not be able to remember details when we come out of it." But to please her, I suggested we try both and see which one would be more suitable for our experiment.

"We can also use the PET scan machine." Sarah suggested, "It will give us a direct view of the working centers, and it would light up brighter after the stimulation."

"Perfect idea." I told her, "As a matter of fact, I am worried about the strong magnetic field from the MRI, and its potential to change the outcome of the experiment. Then we can try both machines and see what we get. Thank you very much for this input."

Sarah then added, "As far as the physics guy, I have one in mind. He looks like a nerd, but he's excellent. He wouldn't mind joining us. Using your name to lure him, we can say we're conducting one of your experiments for the university, and we'll include his name in the paper if it gets published. Of course, he needs to keep it secret, to make sure the results aren't leaked, for the sake of the publication."

"Great." I replied, "Recruiting the computer hacker will be easy too. We can find good ones outside the university. The computer hackers' convention, known as CON, is taking place in Las Vegas next week, the biggest computer hackers convention in the world. Let's attend and try to recruit the best hacker there, and we can start the week after that. I can pay him, or her, from the grant money. It shouldn't be expensive."

"When do we start?" asked Sarah.

"Let's locate all the equipment we need and figure out how we'll sneak it out from those locations every night," I said. "We should locate all the security cameras around the campus, and around the research labs and the MRI and PET scan machines to get around them. Also, please start to work on the physics nerd ASAP."

"Sounds like a plan," Sarah replied.

"And Sarah," I said with a trembling voice as few teardrops appeared in my eyes, "If something happens to me, please publish my data."

Sarah looked worried again and responded, "I promise to do my best, professor, but I hope we can publish this data together, I am not sure why you have this gloomy fear in your heart? Do you know something I don't? Please tell me; we need to be frank about everything."

I answered, "Absolutely not, it is just crucial for me to get this information known, through me or past me, at any cost, and you are my reliable disciple in that matter, to carry the message over, the most important is the data, the message, not me."

I didn't want to share with Sarah one lingering thought that I always had in my mind. I didn't want to scare her. The fact that I'd always believed that I would die during my sleep. In recent weeks, I'd begun to feel that this was more and more likely to happen. That was why I wanted to start the experiment as soon as possible. I felt that time was running out for me somehow. "My theories can't die with me. It would be a disaster. These discoveries could change the world." I was afraid to die before publishing my data. I don't care if I die later. I felt like I had tapped into a forbidden territory or gotten access to classified information that no one else had seen or known before, and the price of that is death. I felt that I was taking a bite from the forbidden apple, from the tree of knowledge. Since I am most vulnerable while asleep, and unfortunately, it is the one thing I, or anyone else to that matter, can't avoid, as we must sleep to stay alive, the simplest way to get rid of me would be during REM sleep, while I am paralyzed and helpless. Just like crashing Super Mario in his game, while on pause, or activating the bad guys, such as Goomba, Gloomba, Anti Guy or Spear Guy, to effectively take care of him until it's game over.

I wondered how many people died during their sleep. Too many, every day, very normal. How many of those were induced by the other reality? To us, it is just another one who dies in his sleep. Another one bites the dust, in his sleep, or should I say, another one bites the dust mites and bed bugs?

CHAPTER 11

What Doesn't Happen in Vegas Also Stays in Vegas

Sarah and I met at the airport, on the way to Las Vegas. She was wearing a sleeveless, light turquoise silk shirt and tight jeans. She looked beautiful, and her attire was so different from her usual university outfits. I felt we were getting closer than ever before. The trip was a great chance to get to know Sarah in her usual casual self.

When we arrived in Vegas, it was nighttime. The weather was sweltering, and the air was stagnant and dry. The environment was festive. I felt things could be done in Vegas that couldn't be done anywhere else. I felt more adventurous. I felt that things that are not permitted anywhere else are allowed in this city. It was the law of that land. The main rule was that there were no rules.

We checked in at the Venetian resort, where the annual hacker convention, CON, would be held for the next three days. We shared adjacent but separate rooms with a closed-door in between. The first thing I wanted to know was whether that door could be opened, but I didn't want to check that right away.

"Why don't we change, and we can walk around and have dinner somewhere?" I suggested.

Sarah said, "Sure."

An hour later, Sarah knocked on the door between our rooms and said, "I'm ready."

I replied, "I've been ready."

Sarah opened the door and came into my room. She was wearing a fancy black dress. Her bare, broad shoulders were shining above the dress, and her beautiful shape was visible underneath the dress. All her curves and every inch of her skin were attractive to me in a crazy way. She looked like an angel in a human outfit, which is much more interesting than an angel in an angel outfit.

I said, "You look gorgeous. I've never seen you like this before. I was missing a lot."

Sarah blushed and looked down as she replied, "Thanks for the compliment."

We strolled around the different hotels, to Paris, New York, and Luxor, walking among crowds of people, all in a festive mood. Was it the hot, dry air? The alcohol? Or the "No rules" rule? I began to think rules are stupid. They tie us in a prison of routine and suffocates us for no reason. We would be much happier without them, like the people in Vegas.

We stopped to eat dinner at a fancy restaurant in Caesars Palace.

I told Sarah, "This trip has made me feel much closer to you."

She replied, "Do you want to be closer?"

"As close as I can be," I said, "As close as you permit me to be. I know that our thoughts are close. Except for a few exceptions, we have the same research goals, and we're both interested in the brain, so we should join forces and be one team."

"And what would be the name of the team?" Sarah asked.

I answered quickly, "Team finding love."

"Woo!" said Sarah with a smile as she appeared pleasantly surprised, "What a surprise. How come a neuroscientist, who has spent all his life in medicine, research, and brain science, talk a real language of love now? How strange?"

I felt a bit challenged and replied without a pause, "For love itself, love is that thing that put us here together without a date. It is the one that created all those effects for us to fall in love. I was missing a big part of my research by missing love. Without experiencing love, the equations would never resolve, and my research would always be incomplete."

Sarah replied, "So you chose me to help you complete your research."

"Yes, exactly," I said quickly without thinking but realized immediately that I just made a blunder. I rushed back saying rapidly, "Sorry, no, you tricked me. It isn't like that at all. See, Sarah, love is never planned. It comes out of nowhere, but always at the right time. No one could see it coming; even Gods cannot plan it. I could have only dreamt of it before. You are, to me, like a dream that was going around inside my brain repeatedly. I saw you in my mind so many times, long before I even saw you. My DNA was searching for your DNA. One moment with you cancels out so many useless years in my life. My entire system was looking for your system. My receptors were waiting to meet your antigens from the beginning. Without you, they would still be empty. Only you can satisfy them because they are specific receptors, destined for your antigens. No one else can fit on them. Without you, I am like an expensive dress that was never worn or a fancy watch that was never set to the right time. Without you, I am like an expensive piece of art that was created and then stored in a basement forever, where nobody saw it, a car that stayed at the dealership forever and never hit the road. Without you, I am like a gourmet food that took a very long time to prepare and was never eaten and finally spoiled and was thrown away in the trash. Without you, and only you, I am useless. By loving you, I found the body that will wear me, the person who will follow the time on my watch, the minds that will appreciate my beautiful art, the driver that will drive me and take me to hit the roads, and the person who will eat me and enjoy eating me and save me from ending up in the trash."

Sarah said, "I didn't, by any means, expect this. I'm surprised. Suddenly, I'm seeing a new person, a lovely person, a loving person. I've never expected these strong emotions to come from you. I always thought neuroscientists were either crazy or very cold people with no emotions."

"That's true," I told her, "Of most scientists, not only neuroscientists. They don't want to include love anywhere in their explanations of science, even though it's all around us, everywhere, in life and nature. We'll be the first scientists to discover the codes for love and include it in our equations. We're the pioneers in this field, and we have to be in love to fully explain it better and better and be able to put it in its proper place alongside the other theories."

Sarah asked, "What do you suggest?"

Pounding with my fist on the table, I said firmly, "We have to start this love experience immediately. I've wasted so much time alone. I'm so deprived of love, deprived of you and only you. You are the therapy to my disorder, the rain that will end my drought. Only you can satisfy my craving, addictive brain to you. Only you can save me from ending up in the trash forever."

"Well, that's a very hot and stormy beginning," said Sarah. "Can we try to cool down a bit and take a little more time?"

"I'm overdue, and we're here now," I replied quickly, "We should capture the opportunity. There is no time; life is very short."

Sarah said, "But I'm not sure I'm ready for this love tsunami. I'd rather take it a step at a time and test the waters first."

At that moment, I felt my heart dropping to my feet, as I tried to figure out why she was hesitant? Did she not like me? Was it the age difference? Is there somebody else in her life? Or maybe there had been someone, and she wasn't ready to open herself for a new experience yet. Was her reluctance only a matter of time or permanent?

Please allow me to prove my love to you," I told Sarah. "Consider this conversation like an appetizer, and the main course will come later. I'll try to change anything you want me to switch to win your heart."

Sarah asked, "Do you think you can let your research go and live a different life, a simple life of the here and now, a material life like everyone else? Would you be happy?"

I said, "I'd become a different person then. I consider myself a prophet who was given a message to deliver to everyone, a message that can change their lives. Somehow, I feel that I was chosen to receive this message, and I must deliver it. Through me, comes an opportunity to finally decipher reality and allow people to understand their true identity and true reality. I could only give that up under two circumstances, if I lose my mind for some reason, or if you want me to give it all up. But as long as I have my mental capacity, I could only give this up for you."

Sarah shook her head and said, "No, I'd love for you to continue, and I'm also in it with you. It was just a thought. Why don't we live a simpler life like most other people? Live for the day, work for pay, and gossip to waste time, play bridge or backgammon, and pay attention to the useless details people worry about every day. Party and travel and watch useless news and TV episodes."

I said, "That's not us, Sarah. That's a waste of life, and it would never make us happy. We have a mission, a goal in mind, and that goal may change the world around us. I don't care about my own life, except for two things, your love, if you share it with me, and my research. I really don't want to die before these two goals are accomplished."

We left the restaurant, and my heart was still heavy, stuck around my feet and I felt like I was dragging it behind me, between my shoes, and it felt like I was chained to a bowling ball, stuck to the ground.

I wondered, "Why does love always do that? It goes around and around, to one lover at a time sequentially, never fully satisfied, and never satisfies both lovers at the same time. It is always looking for someone else, or something else, other than the one who is available and ready. The Goddess of love must be a funny one, always looking for excitement. She enjoys playing around with people's hearts for her entertainment and amusement. Even when She finally finds the perfect match, it doesn't last a good while. Time comes soon enough and kills everything. It kills love first and then, kills us later. To keep love alive, we should never reach that final state of satisfaction together. Instead, we should keep longing for it and dreaming about each other longer. The faster we reach that final moment of satisfaction, the quicker we'd lose love, and then we'd need a new goal. Love is like a hummingbird, going from one flower to another spreading love from his tongue, causing momentary climax for the flowers, and then going away and moving on to another flower. It could never stay longer than a few moments, and we live only for those few moments. Without the dose of that momentary love, we'd go to waste. Our entire life value would be in vain. Just like when the hummingbird misses a flower and never comes back around again for it, and its nectar keeps accumulating inside of it without appreciation, without pleasure.

At that moment, I gathered myself quietly and told myself, "It isn't over yet. I will win Sarah's heart with my persistence and will prove to her that I am worthy of sharing her love and life too."

Many ideas came to my head simultaneously. What is the plan now, showing all these emotions could adversely affect the outcome? I look like I am basically drooling for her love, and I realized that this might scare her. I thought I should calm down and appear more laid back as if I don't care, but I didn't know how to do that?

Back at the hotel, Sarah felt my gloominess, and she said goodnight briefly and closed the middle door again. I almost cried when I heard her locking the door up from her side. I felt like a beggar who was turned away when he was starving and genuinely desperate. Why did she lock the door? Was I that bad? That really hurt my feelings.

The next morning, I brought coffee and knocked on Sarah's door. She opened so many locks before the door finally opened.

Sarah said, "Good morning. Did you sleep well?"

"Not really," I told her. "I was kind of distraught, not sure why. I kept on having nightmares, one after the other"

"What did you dream of?" Sarah asked.

I said, "I saw myself being thrown away in a huge trash bin, and I was rotting away, and all the while, other people were still being thrown in the trash with me. I heard a voice saying, 'You guys came from the trash, and now you deserve to go back to the trash. It's your fault that nobody liked you. You were no good, unappealing. We spent so much time and effort to make you guys worthy, but you failed us. Your proper place is in the trash now.' And as the trash was being sucked in to be destroyed, I saw you looking down on me. I raised my arm for you to pick me up. You tried hard to pull me out of the trash, but it was too late. The pull of the garbage truck was much stronger than you. I dropped into a swirling; bottomless black hole full of trash."

Sarah frowned as she said, "That was a horrible nightmare." But she did not appear genuinely concerned.

"Indeed," I said with open eyes full of new hopes, "But now that I see your beautiful face; it's a new day and a new chance for me."

We went down to the CON, the computer hacker's convention, the biggest in the entire world. We walked through room after room of lengthy presentations about new methods and devices, and we didn't understand anything. Our goal was to try to pick up the best hacker available for our research project. We heard a lot of good names in the business, but by far, the most famous name among the hackers was Mike Hachey, also known as "Mike, the hacker." Everybody concurred that he was outstanding, and he also had a background in medical hacking tactics, like hacking medical records and hospital information.

We saw Mike for the first time from far away. He was on stage, speaking about hacking medical information and tampering with health care reports, basically changing medical diagnoses for insurance fraud purposes. I was shocked to know that this could even be done. The whole conference was shocking, and the biggest shock was that there was a worldwide annual conference to discuss these issues publicly.

After his presentation, Sarah and I approached Mike at the podium and asked him to meet with us privately for a business deal. Mike had a very suspicious personality; he appeared paranoid and greeted us with extreme caution. He only agreed to meet us in the lobby of another hotel, later that evening.

We met with Mike in the lobby of the Bellagio. He was disguised in a Hawaiian shirt, a straw hat, and sunglasses, and he was smoking a pipe. "Keep in mind," he said, "That I charge for this initial consultation, including my time getting dressed up for this meeting."

"But who told you to dress up?" I asked him.

Mike said, "Those are the rules of the game. If you want to play it right, it must be this way, by my rules. Take it or leave it."

"Okay, okay," I said. "Great start. Can you give us an idea of what your fees will be?"

"Depending on the mission," Mike said. "You pay for my time, all preparations, including dressing up, phone calls, even your conversation with me at the podium is also included in the calculations. Any contact is one hundred dollars, minimum, no matter how brief, and after the initial contact fee, every fifteen minutes is another hundred dollars. Now, explain the project quickly, and I'll tell you how much I will charge."

Sarah and I explained the project from beginning to end to Mike. It took a while to get him to understand the information correctly.

Mike said with a look of amusement, "So you want me to hack people while sleeping and see if I can reach a source or a computer program behind their reality, like a server, and try to identify it. And if I find a server or a source, try to corrupt the data, cause glitches in the program, for us to see how that would affect or change our current reality universe? Is that right?"

Sarah and I replied at the same time, "Yes, exactly!"

Mike looked at Sarah and asked her, "And what's your role in this project?"

"I'm a partner in this research with Dr. Zachary, and I'll be alternating with him as the subject of the experiment," said Sarah.

Mike said with wide-open eyes, "So, I'll hack you as well while you're sleeping?"

I said quickly, "No, no, no, you will only hack me. It's not necessary for you to hack Sarah."

"Could there be different sources, different realities, behind you two?" asked Mike. "Don't you want to discover that reality too?"

"Well, that makes sense," Sarah replied as she looked pleased to be in the center of attention.

"First," I said in a loud voice, "We'll start the experiment with me and see how it goes. I don't think it will be necessary for you to hack Sarah ever, but we'll decide about that later."

I felt jealous for the first time in my life. I felt the need to protect Sarah's brain from this parasite. If anyone should hack her brain, it should be me, and only me, her brain needs to open only to me. I didn't want a sneaky guy like Mike the hacker tampering with her brain or her emotions. At that moment, I hated the guy so much. I couldn't believe we had to deal with him. He treated me kind of rough, and at the same time, he was very gentle with Sarah. When he answered me, he looked angry, and when he looked at Sarah, his eyes glared, and his mood totally changed.

Mike said, "For such a project if you reach a conclusion or not, I get twenty-five grand."

I said, "Fifteen."

"Twenty-two."

"Twenty is my final offer," I said, "And I'll pay you from the research grant."

"Deal, but I also have two more conditions," said Mike.

"What now?"

"I also want to be part of the experiment, meaning, I will also be put to sleep, and I'll record my own data. And my name should also go on the published paper."

Sarah said, "That's great. We'll have an independent observer."

"Okay," I told Mike. "We'll get you a university ID badge as a research associate. I'll contact you next week."

"Only through secure email," Mike said.

Mike looked at Sarah and said, "See you later then." He didn't even look at me.

Sarah and I walked back to the Venetian hotel.

I asked her, "What do you think?"

"I think he's perfect for the job, and he's also motivated by the project, to the point that he wants to record his own data, which I found remarkable. A bit expensive, but he'll do the job, hopefully."

"I just don't like his personality," I told her, "He's arrogant, paranoid, not friendly at all, and obnoxious."

Sarah said, "As long as he does the job. I don't know if we'd ever find a friendly hacker. Mike may be better than others. We're talking about borderline criminals here."

I said, "You're right. But please, don't let him hack you. He's dangerous. He might make you do things that you don't want to do. If anything, I should be the only one who can do that, for security reasons."

I thought to myself, "If only I could hack her brain, and make her fall for me right away. That would be great. But no, she should reach that conclusion herself."

Back at the hotel, after saying goodnight, Sarah closed the door, but this time she didn't lock it. I was thrilled and encouraged. Did she just forget? Or was she implicitly inviting me to knock on the door, or knock it off entirely from existence?

After fifteen minutes, I knocked on the door. "Sarah, are you sleeping?"

Sarah said, "Not yet."

I asked, "Can I come in?"

"Wait for a second," she replied.

Then Sarah opened the door and came into my room. She wore a silk pajama, with silk shorts and a transparent robe. She looked so beautiful that I could not believe I could exist in the same room with this divine, gorgeous being. Her smell was inviting, and her softness was exactly what I'd been dreaming of.

I opened a bottle of wine, poured two glasses, and turned on some of the on-demand music.

Without even asking, I stretched my hand to Sarah, to dance.

We stood up and started swaying with the music softly. With one hand around her waist, and the other embracing her beautiful hand, we got closer and closer, moving in a slow rhythm. I felt every curve in her body with my body and hands. Her soft skin and touch drove me crazy.

In slow motion, spontaneously, our lips touched, and I wanted to squeeze her inside of me. *"Come in, my dear Sarah. You do not need an invitation. This is your home, your new country, and you can do whatever you want with it. The great wall around the city has fallen, and the city is open wide and ready for the new triumphant conqueror. All systems are ready for the new ruler and his new rules. Please have mercy on me."*

Those moments were magic to me. They felt like an eternity. *This is what we're born to experience. This is exactly what we're born to do and to be. It is not sleep then; It is love.*

Thank God, I'm not in the trash anymore, I was so close. And the relics went on.

> Dance me to your beauty with a burning violin
> Dance me through the panic until I'm gath-
> ered safely in
> Lift me like an olive branch and be my
> homeward dove
> Dance me to the end of love
> Dance me to the end of love
>
> Oh, let me see your beauty when the wit-
> nesses are gone
> Let me feel you moving like they do in Babylon
> Show me slowly what I only know the limits of
> And dance me to the end of love

After the dance, Sarah said she was tired and wanted to sleep, and she rushed back to her room. I stood still for a while, not understanding what was going on or what should happen next. This time Sarah left the door open.

Ok, great, what am I supposed to do now? Why did she leave the door open? Did she forget?

I sat on the floor near the door, thinking for a while. Nobody had taught me what to do next. Should I enter her room and beg her for more love, more time? Enter the room and sleep next to her on her bed without an invitation? Sit here and wait for her invitation? Or go to sleep in my bed? I felt my brain aching from thinking about what to do; this decision was much more complicated than neuroscience to me.

I decided to stay where I was for a while, until I fell asleep on the floor near the door, like a polite dog, very loyal to his master, and waiting for her approval to enter and play.

In the middle of the night, I saw Sarah looking at me on the floor and smiling, kissed me on my forehead, and covered me with a warm blanket. Was that a dream? I also saw myself crawling on four limbs like a loving pet dog, towards Sarah's bed and licking her hands, feet, cheeks, ears, and lips and all over. Was that also a dream?

That night, I had many pleasant dreams. In the one I remembered most clearly, I was turned into a piece of art, a naked statue, like Michelangelo's David, standing in the center of a large display hall in a very famous museum, and lots of people were rushing and standing in line to see me, and I was feeling their admiration, and enjoying it. I was feeling very worthy and valuable. I was a centerpiece of the utmost beauty and importance.

The next morning, I woke up to find myself on the floor, holding on tight to a pillow, like I was holding somebody, without a blanket. I peeked into Sarah's room, and she was sleeping deeply, holding another pillow tightly.

I arranged for flowers and breakfast to be sent to Sarah's room, and after they were delivered, I went into her room with coffee. The flowers were located by the window, where the soft morning light shone through, reflecting on Sarah's hair and beautiful skin and her bare shoulder with the strap of her pajama hanging down to her mid-arm. This scene was the most beautiful image I'd ever witnessed in my entire life. It felt like seeing a divine deity, like Aphrodite waking up in the morning, and all I needed to do is to bow to her beauty and worship.

"What a beautiful morning," I said, "Being here next to you. This is the most beautiful morning I ever recall having in my entire life. If only those aches would go away. I slept on the floor all night."

"Why did you sleep on the floor?" asked Sarah.

"I was frozen, not sure what to do next after you left me last night. I thought of many options, but only dreamt of doing any of them, and finally, in the end, I did nothing at all. Nothing in my dreams and nothing in reality either. I froze in my place until the morning, like one of Pompeii volcano victims when Mount Vesuvius erupted and turned people into stone. I wish I'd had more courage."

Sarah asked, "Courage to do what?"

"To do what I was dreaming of."

"It looks like you dream a lot," said Sarah.

"Yes," I said, "Since reality didn't grant me the privileges I wanted, I could only dream. I realized that I could do a lot of things with you in my dreams, without even asking your permission. I hope you don't object to this either."

Sarah said, "No objections, but it depends on the dream. What did you dream of?"

"Excluding the dreams that you were in, the most important one I remember that I was posing as a naked statue in a famous museum, and lots of people were admiring me."

"With a leaf on," Sarah asked, "Or without?"

"Without," I replied.

Sara laughed hard. "Oh no, I don't object at all to have been there, watching the historical moment. Was touch allowed?"

"No, no touching was allowed. It was the museum rules, and they were very strict about it, absolutely no touching."

Sarah said, "Sometimes I wonder where you get all this romance from."

"I didn't know this about myself either," I told her, "Until you came into my picture frame. You opened a deep well in me that I never knew existed before. Like one of Yellowstone national park's geysers that have been covered for ages and now is constantly erupting nonstop. I feel emotions that I never dreamt of before, sweeping me and my personality aside, like a fast-flowing river depositing my insignificant identity self on its banks, like debris. I can feel it erasing my core self and lifting a sacred part of me to a higher place. A place that I've never been or seen before. Soaring above everything that used to matter to me before, above my interests, and even above my own self."

"By the way, what time is the flight back?" Sarah asked.

I looked at my watch and said, "Shoot! It's in one hour."

Unfortunately, we had to hurry to check out and catch the return flight home. I left my sweet dreams in Vegas. So many pleasant dreams to store in my memory, and so many delightful things I dreamt of doing and never did any of them after all, but still gave me lots of pleasure. I guessed, what does not happen in Vegas, also, stays in Vegas.

CHAPTER 12

The Experiment

Two weeks after we returned from Vegas, I received the NIH grant money and started planning for the research to begin. I had the surgical procedure to implant the high-frequency deep stimulation electrodes directly in my brain, done reluctantly by one of my neurosurgery colleagues. I secretly told him about our project, and he was convinced of its importance. He agreed to do it off the record, with no documentation, after making me sign several consents. Those electrodes had very tiny infusion catheters to inject small quantities of stimulating neurotransmitters, for direct biochemical stimulation of the brain centers. Among some of those neurotransmitters were proteins like, the Brain-Derived-Neurotrophic Factor or BDNF, dopamine, acetylcholine, and serotonin, which we were able to get small quantities of, from our research labs.

I needed a face traction mask, made of steel iron, to fix my head during the experiment, like the ones used in head and neck cancer radiation therapy. The laser and the TMS must go precisely through the mouth, directly to the brain stem region, right behind the pharynx. I refused to let Sarah get that procedure done, and she was okay with that. She thought I must be crazy to try all these new techniques without previous controlled clinical trials to prove their safety. Sarah opposed the idea that I'd go through this all at once. She said it could be dangerous, but she agreed later that it was the best way to get good results quickly.

The goal of the experiment was to induce deeper phases of sleep and REM sleep, and for a much longer time, using the neurotransmitters. At the same time, inhibit the conscious brain deeper and activate the hippocampus memory center to remember those dreams vividly. Sarah would be like the pilot of the experiment, while the physics guy attempts to trace the electromagnetic waves coming in or going out of my brain, and Mike, the hacker, attempts to hack any computer system/s beyond those electromagnetic waves, like a server, or a source of information system.

The NIH grant was for studying the effects of longer deep sleep and longer REM sleep time on life expectancy in fruit flies. The real research we had in mind was on human subjects or "human fruit flies." — a slight deviation from the original protocol.

We got the IV melatonin and Propofol, the TMS coil, and the laser stimulation machine, the high-frequency deep brain stimulation equipment, the EEG and EMG machines, IV poles, and a sophisticated vital signs monitors, like the ones used in intensive care units for monitoring blood pressure, pulse and oxygen levels in the blood. We transferred everything to the PET scan suite. We could not do this in the MRI room because of MRI's strong magnetic force. The first day, it took us quite a long time to finally set up everything in place and begin conducting the experiment.

I told Sarah, "We have to figure out a way to store all this equipment here for the next few days or weeks. We can't repeat this effort every time. We've put in more than four hours' worth of work already. Also, since the research grant is approved for animal research and not human research, we need to be secretive about what we're doing."

Sarah introduced me to the physics guy that she'd recruited from the department of theoretical physics. His nickname was Neon, and he was known to possess an extraordinary sense of detecting the direction in which electromagnetic waves were going or coming from, like Wi-Fi waves, for example. He had this ability to detect the presence, location, and direction of different sorts of waves. During his research, he was able to develop very sophisticated and advanced devices and techniques to detect and photograph those waves and locate their origin. It was known about him that he was able to take pictures of things like Bluetooth waves, and Wi-Fi waves around campuses and in Starbucks, for example, and identify their source origins at times.

"Perfect man for the job," I said.

Mike, the hacker, showed up in a detective outfit, wearing a detective's hat and an overcoat. He brought a massive computer, the size of a small deep freezer, with several antennas and satellite dishes attached to it.

"Now," I said, "It looks like we're finally ready to start."

I still had to keep an eye on Mike and keep him away from Sarah as much as possible. The problem was that I would be in a deep sleep state and wouldn't be able to monitor him. I certainly didn't want that issue to bother me, because that distraction itself might interfere with the results or prevent the deep connections from happening. I had to let it go for the time being. I believed Sarah loves me and would never fall for a devious guy like Mike.

It felt like directing a movie, and we were finally ready to start shooting. Act one, scene one, take one action!

"Ready everyone?" I asked.

And they all replied, "Yes, professor."

Wearing a surgical mask, gloves, and a medical gown, Sarah sat next to me, by the PET scan table. I had the IV fluid running in my veins, and the direct brain catheter port deep inside my brain. I had the iron traction mask on, with my mouth open wide. Around me were the laser stimulation machine, the TMS machine, and the high-frequency deep brain stimulation machine. I was also connected directly to the EEG monitor and the EMG monitor, as well as the vital signs monitors.

Sarah asked, "Ready to experience reality, professor?"

I said, "Not really, I was hoping for you and me to live in another reality. A simpler reality where love goes on forever and time never kills it. An everlasting, eternal love that's above space-time and is not affected by either."

I held Sarah's hand tightly and said as a tear rolled down my face and across the iron mask, "By the way, if anything happens to me, remember I love you."

Sarah was injecting the melatonin through the IV cannula directly in my veins, and the neurotransmitters directly in my brain. As I was dozing off, I heard myself mumbling, "If something happens to me, please publish my data."

We repeated the experiment day after day, with the same procedure. We also tried using Propofol, and the results were mostly the same.

Sarah's turn to sleep was the third time around. Her experiment was done without the direct deep brain stimulation, or the face traction mask, just using the external laser and TMS stimulation. I tried to keep Mike, the hacker, away that night. I told him, "I'm giving you paid time off." But he showed up unexpectedly as if he intended to hack Sarah's brain for his own interest and hidden motives.

When Mike showed up that night, I asked him, "What are you doing here?"

He answered, "What do you mean?"

"I told you to stay off tonight," I said.

"I do not want to be paid for doing nothing; besides it is crucial for me to record Sarah's experience for the sake of accurate data collection. Sarah wanted me to do so."

"I never knew that you were so keen on the experiment all of a sudden now."

"I don't understand you; don't you want the best data available after all this effort?"

At this moment, Sarah entered the room and heard us arguing loudly.

She said, "Guys, cool down; what do you think he can do, professor?"

At that moment, I wanted to shout, "Because you're mine, only mine, please understand." but I couldn't say any of that. Instead, I looked sharply at Mike and said, "Ok, but I will be monitoring everything you do all the time."

He replied, "Sure, I am not doing anything wrong anyway."

During the fifth session, we tried the experiment on Mike, the hacker, himself, as he requested, but we could not use his equipment. We repeated the experiment eleven times with the same order and recorded our data immediately after coming back from sleep, putting together the imaging and tracking information from Neon and the hacking data from Mike.

We went through different pathways; different alternate universes, that were all available to us. Recorded by Mike and photographed by Neon, we were able to weave the nature of some of those universes.

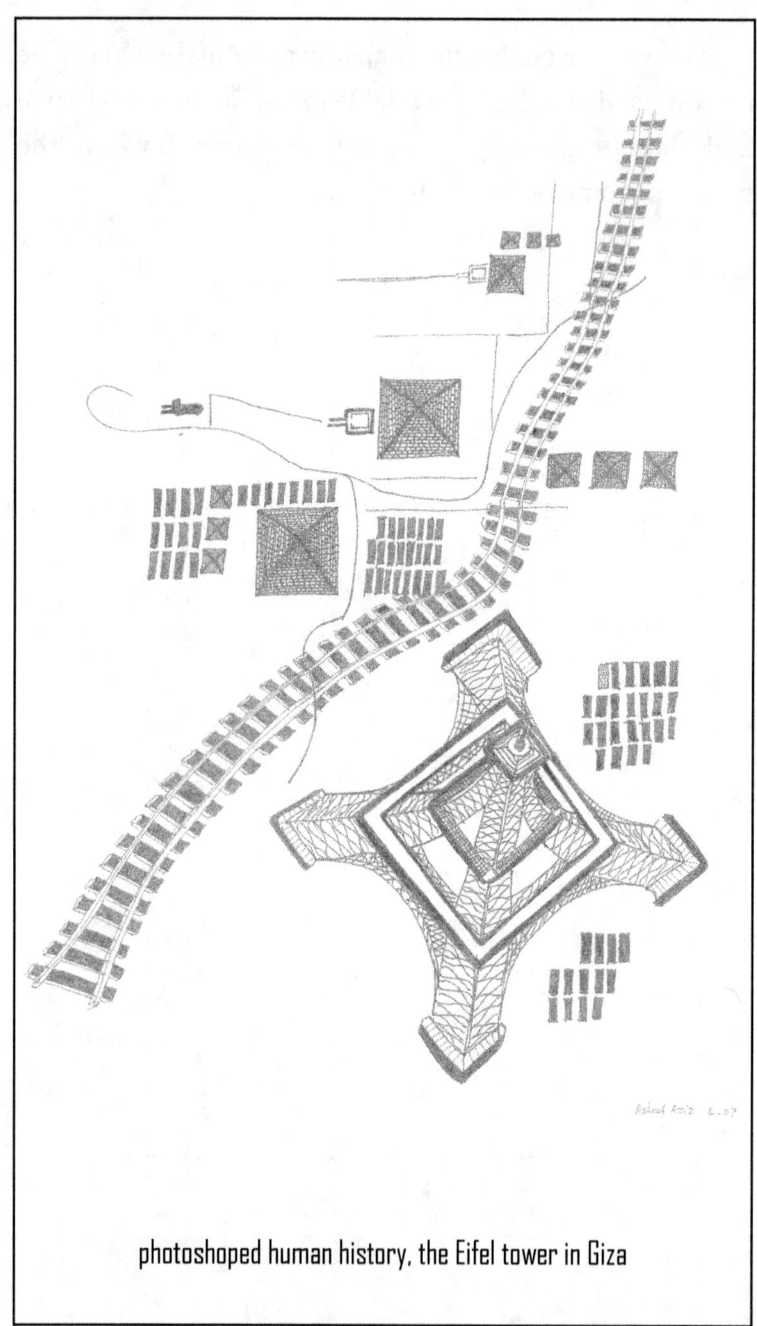

photoshoped human history, the Eifel tower in Giza

The Alternate Universe

Universe A: The Digital Picture Frame Universe

The first time around, after I went asleep, I experienced myself as a conscious living character in a digital picture frame universe. A rather simple experience, with me and the universe around me, was wholly represented in the digital images. The images were changing successively with a very tiny time scale in between them; the scale of Planck time difference (the smallest possible quantum of time). The images could go forward in time or backward in time or in a random shuffled fashion. In the case of the universe I was in, the images were going forward, giving me the perception of time passing. Each successive image was very minutely, morphologically different from the one before. I and everyone around me, were conscious characters inside the digital picture, observing the entire universe around us and perceiving it as a real 3D universe, with a massive amount of digital details and megapixels.

I remembered appreciating the fact that this universe was organized forward in time and not backward or in a random fashion. Imagine living in a random picture frame sequence universe on a shuffle mode? An option available with most of the current commercial digital picture frames. One picture, when you were five years old, and the next, when you're married and have children, and next, a photo when you were born, and another on top of Mount Everest in your youth. It would result in a very confusing universe, and it would not make sense to us. That kind of perceived reality would be dizzying and would drive us crazy — a very complicated universe to imagine; even in fiction or movies.

In a backward sequence digital picture frame universe, we would experience life going backwards, like in the movie "The Curious Case of Benjamin Button" with the difference that this backward time experience would apply to everyone, not just Benjamin Button. In that universe, usual life would start with death and ends with birth for everybody. It would be a better universe since everything would get better and better as we age. We'd get younger and healthier as we age, until we eventually enter our mother's womb and get reduced further to one cell, then divide to an egg and a sperm. In that universe, one may not know his birth parents until the end of his time, then, everyone would know later, where the sperm came from, and who was his true mother and father. That universe would start first, by knowing the caregivers at the end of life first, maybe the children, and lastly get to know the parents towards the beginning of life at the end.

In the going forward digital picture frame universe, like our current universe, our brain remembers the past by remembering the prior frames and what they looked like before the present moment. In a backward timeframe universe, we would remember the future instead of remembering the past. There would be no possible past or future memory in the random digital picture frame universe. It would be hard to figure out how memory would function, or time perception would be, in the random digital picture frame universe, it would resemble fragmented dreams.

It seemed to me that periods of our history, and past civilizations, could have been edited in or out and we don't know how things came to be? Perhaps we just found their pictures present, and we don't know how they got there. For example, Atlantis could have existed, but it could have been mostly edited out from the frames, either by mistake or intentionally. Take the Sphinx as another example, suddenly, it appeared in the pictures, with no detailed prior successive frames that explain how it got there. In other words, we could be missing periods of history that were edited out and could be looking at another history that was edited in, like a photo-shopped, edited history, and possibly photo-shopped, edited present.

The digital picture frame universe could have been a representation of an ancestor simulation too.

Universe B: The Digital Hologram, Virtual Reality Universe

In another episode, I experienced myself in another universe, that looked like a digital hologram universe.

In a conventional hologram, all the picture data are encrypted on a flat 2D background film that contains all the information that's projected to a 3D domain, usually a dark space. Behind the film is a source of light, usually a laser light beam that produces the holographic projection in front of the film. The images in the hologram are like shadows that your hand can go through, but in that universe, they appeared very real to me and every other character living inside the hologram.

In a holographic universe, subjects like me, are living inside the projection as conscious 3D characters, seeing the universe around us from inside, and we only exist inside the hologram and have no idea what exists outside the hologram. We are even unaware that we live inside a hologram, because this was our only experience, just like fish in deep water, they know no other reality other than the water around them.

The cosmic microwave background radiation (CMB) that was created after the Big Bang was represented here as the holographic film that has all the data ingrained on it. Scientists tell us that before the CMB, light could not escape, and the universe was dark. There were no atoms, and electrons were stuck to protons, and light could not escape. Later, when atoms formed, it allowed light to travel away, and then there was light. The CMB happened after the initial rapid expansion of the universe called "cosmic inflation," after which, light waves were able to exit and travel and be seen and detected. As a matter of fact, it is still traveling to us straight from that moment till now, for 13.7 billion years. That CMB radiation is part of what gives us the hissing sound and the fuzzy image that we used to see in the old analog TV sets after programs had ended for the day and there was no reception. We still can hear that hissing sound now. Was that the sound of a projector I was hearing?

In a digital holographic universe, the CMB must be the film where all the information is stored, and the energy source must have traveled through it to give us the holographic reality. Before the CMB, there was mostly darkness and void, as reality only existed after the film, not before. An outside observer can see the hologram as a hologram and can pass through the projected images like walking through clouds, but for us and the others inside the hologram, we see it as a solid reality thanks to our brains that perceive it that way.

I was thinking at that time; if we can travel to the CMB and take a closer look at the data, we may be able to decipher the information and discover what will happen to our universe, and us, later. And further back, if we can go through the CMB, we could pass straight to the source of projection and discover who is behind the projector.

The vastness of the universe is only an illusion; it is just a projection in a digital hologram. Our universe is not vast, after all. Also, time is not that long either. It's only projected over a short time, and we perceive the universe that vast and time that long thanks to our brains. I always thought that the universe is too vast to be real. For economic reasons, the vastness of space-time is better explained as an illusion, or a simulation, rather than a physical reality. Physical matter in the digital holographic universe is nearly nothing, as everything is digital bits, and from inside the projection, it would calculate to close to zero amount of physical matter, just like what we observe in our universe.

Now because of our scientific advances and discoveries, we can see the film that our reality details are encrypted on and can hear the projector that is projecting our reality. Otherwise, we would have never comprehended what is going on.

Universe C: Second Life Universe and Pets Second Life Universe

Fourth time around, Sarah experienced what looked like a second life universe. *Second Life* is an online virtual reality world where users create virtual characters, representations of themselves, called avatars. They can interact with places, objects, and other avatars within the program. They can travel and explore the world around them, meet others, and socialize. Those avatars can shop, and trade virtual property and services with one another. The program has its own virtual currency, which is exchangeable with real world currency. The avatars can fall in love and get married. It is a computer-generated, interactive 3D game, that is dependent on, and actively interacting with real living players, and what happens in the program is entirely reliant on the choices of the actual players, not the avatars.

Sarah experienced her universe reality as similar to a second life reality game program, with one significant difference, is that, when users choose their avatars in the current usual game program, they exist immediately with their previously selected features and images, and they stay forever in those images without change, they do not age or grow. Instead, in Sarah's second life reality program, when avatars are chosen, they had to be born first in the program, grow gradually, and eventually, die inside the program. The program predates the individual avatars and continues past them, and it is okay. It's just how the rules of the program were designed.

In the *Second Life* universe, Sarah experienced that we exist as conscious avatars in a virtual reality web-based program that was created by many different individuals at different times. It started very small and simple and got much bigger and more complex with time. Just like humanity started with a humble beginning and got much more prominent and complicated to the degree we see today. Like the complexity that we might expect to see for the current *Second Life* program to be in a thousand or ten thousand years from now.

Sarah thought when experiencing life in that program, it was also possible that the creators of reality second life universe, intended to create a special program for virtual pets, instead of having real pets. In that virtual second life pet program, pets are created individually by different users based on their preferences. Pets could be animals or avatars, but only avatars became conscious of their nature.

Birth starts when one of the users of *Second Life* desires to have a new pet. They click on the order icon, and then the program searches for a woman or a couple inside the program, who are ready and capable of having a baby. Whether these women or couples desire to have it or not, sometimes babies just come anyway. The baby comes through them but doesn't belong to them. The parents only serve as protectors and guardians to guarantee the baby's well-being and survival.

Once a baby is born, (which is a random event in the game world, as orders do not specify parents or location) there are only two necessities that the baby or the pet is required to do to stay alive. Those two necessities are eating and sleeping. Eating allows them to grow bigger and perform activities to entertain their creators and to be able to reproduce later. The virtual pets get their food supply rather than depend on their owners to feed them. Imagine having pets that you don't have to worry about feeding because they work to produce their own food, a more comfortable and more economical way of having pets and enjoying them better. The second necessity is sleeping, which allows for essential downloads and upgrades. The energy supply of the program is self-sustained, powered from the electromagnetic energy emitted from its characters, as an eventual byproduct of their food intake. Eventually, everyone must die in submission to the rules of the program.

Another obligation, which is not a necessity but highly desired and is deeply embedded in all the pets and avatars' life code program, is the urge to reproduce and conceive new members to maintain the ability to create more pets and more avatars whenever the users want to. The program allows the users to create a new pet/avatar whenever they desire to, and that's why there are more couples available than there are possible babies. That's why some couples still do not conceive even though they make every effort to have a baby. Sometimes because they don't want to conceive; other times, due to a physical barrier to conception, or sometimes, simply, because the program doesn't have a ready customer, at the same moment that the couple is trying to conceive. The longer the couples try, and the more they persist, the better their chance to get new babies, but nothing is guaranteed.

The morphology and behavior of the new pet, or the newborn avatar, is determined by the desire of the user/s but also restricted by the genetic code of their parents. The users are still able to choose from many morphological options but within the characteristics of the genetic code of the parents. It's like choosing from different clothes within a category of choices.

The avatars perceive themselves, and the environment and everything else within the program as a real, living reality mastered by their brains. It is the only reality that their brains know and able to perceive inside the program. They are born in the program, grow up in the program, and later, die in the program. Unfortunately, the avatars acquired artificial intelligence as time went by, most likely accidentally, and started exploring what is behind their reality game. They do not have the slightest idea what life is like, or what the rules are, outside their second life game program. The avatars also do not know who the real players are, and not aware either that those players determine most of their major life events for them.

Universe D: The Digital Video Game Universe, The Super Mario Universe.

Next, it was my turn, and I experienced one of my favorite universes out of all the alternate universes we experienced, a universe that looked like a video game, and I looked like Super Mario inside that universe. In the Super Mario universe, me, or let's better say "Super Mario", sees everything around him as real, but when he tries to understand the physics of the world surrounding him, he discovers that his world has a digital nature, based on zeros and ones, and that includes him as well. Everything in his universe is a code that was made of zeros and ones and propagated to more and more complex codes that dictate his nature and the nature of the universe around him. He discovers that he is stuck around the middle of the program code, and it's tough to go far in, or far out, from the middle of the code.

He's practically stuck like a prisoner in space and time, or space-time, as he is very tiny, and his time frame is very minute, in a vastly written program that spans billions and billions of codes beyond his time and space frames. If he goes backward or forward, if he zooms in or out of his position, he only goes a minimal distance and a small quantum of time in a vast ocean of information and codes. If he were able to zoom in all the way, he would get to the zeros and ones, but not sure how he would recognize them or see them, as they are virtual. On the other hand, if he could zoom out all the way, he could see the future of his program.

All the information is written and is available, but it's played one piece at a time, which is his present time. If he could read into the program, he would be able to know the rules of his universe, the entire story, the whole script of the game. It is almost like a movie written digitally on a DVD. The whole movie is available on the disc. The information is always available and present on the disc drive, but it's played out in a specific sequence, one digital frame at a time, and we perceive time passing only because of the playing action of the game, one frame at a time.

In the Super Mario universe, nature and reality propagate as he goes, and none of it existed until he decides to go, or one of the individuals living along with him in the game decides to go or is already present there to observe it. Reality is created as they go like a red carpet rolled out in front of a famous actress as she walks. Since the program is massive and has so many individuals, their reality is also substantial. That means Australia, for example, must exist, even though Super Mario has never seen it and has never been there, as long as someone in the program lives there or has visited that country before and knows it is there. However, it's a different story for the places that no one has ever been before, like Alpha Centauri (our closest star, besides the Sun), for example. If someone decides to go to Alpha Centauri, only then it will exist. Reality is created as Super Mario, or the other characters in the program are there to observe it.

If Super Mario decides to go to the end of the universe, he will appear on the opposite side of the universe, just like in the video game. The program loops back from one end to the other, and that's one theory we can test experimentally. We can send astronauts to the end of the universe, for example, from the right side, and see them pop out from the left side. Also, similarly, if someone goes up to the upper end of the universe, he would appear back from the bottom. If that happens, it will prove the theory correct.

In the Super Mario universe, Super Mario has choices as to where he wants to go, but once he decides to go there, reality is determined for him. The rules of the game are also written such that characters like Super Mario and Luigi are born into the program, grow older, live, reproduce, and eventually die, unlike the commercial video game, where Super Mario exists as a Super Mario from the beginning and stays forever as Super Mario, unchanged.

The role that Super Mario plays in the video game universe is trivial. He is just another mortal character, who is born into the program, grows, lives and wants to reproduce, and eventually dies in the program. He must sleep to be programmed, upgraded, and updated, every night, to be able to continue to perform his functions properly, and possibly in order to generate power for the program to go on and on forever. Once he ages, Super Mario becomes less efficient at fighting the bad guys, and he also becomes less useful and less flexible to adapt to new changes, until eventually, a final blow from one of the bad guys knocks him dead. With no extra life available for him anymore, he dies in the program and the game is over for him, but still not game over yet. The program continues and waits for another new and improved Super Mario to be born and continue to play. There is nothing immortal in the program, except for the rules and codes; otherwise, everything else comes and goes.

Inside the program, Super Mario sees himself as real. He perceives the program around him, with all its morphology and terrain, as his vast universe. His brain and his sensory organs are designed to help him make his way around in the program successfully with ease. He eats and drinks to get the energy to grow and reproduce and make his way within the program, self-sustained.

Super Mario is programmed to acquire material things around him, to survive, and he becomes more powerful by acquiring goods and money and other stuff. He is mostly distracted by the reality around him. It's continuously keeping him busy, so he doesn't have time to think of himself, his nature, or the nature of his program? What might the real reality behind his existence be? The program keeps him occupied and distracted so he would continue with the program agenda as it is. The game must go on.

In my case, I, or Super Mario acquired knowledge and became conscious along the way somehow, acquired an AI. This consciousness most likely developed accidentally and was not intentional. He started to think of his nature and reality and eventually discovered that he's a part of a vast computer program, a game. He and his entire universe are simply codes, and his morphology and the images that he sees around him are images projected on a flat screen, like a computer screen, or a monitor, or a hologram. His brain is what makes him perceive that he is living a true life here, and everything seems real around him when it's all only a computer projection. He sees, feels, hears, touches, and smells everything around him as if it were real when it is all just images on a computer screen, and he is a part of the whole thing.

Super Mario has no chance to exit the program or survive outside of it because he doesn't have a physical body. He is just a code translated into images on a screen, and he only can exist on that screen. Even after Super Mario discovered that he's inside the game and he's part of the program, he soon realized that he can only exist within the program. He and his universe could quickly vanish if the program is terminated for some reason. For example, if somebody decides to turn off the game, his whole universe would be gone, unless that someone remembers to save it before the shutdown.

While there, I imagined, one day, Super Mario, decides to hack his game program, and try to get to know the entire code, and attempts to decipher it or change it. He tries to make contact with the programmer or the game player/s and take pictures of him/them if possible. He would like to let him/them know that he exists in the program and that he acquired AI and all this knowledge. He tries to tell them that he has feelings and emotions, and he is a significant being living inside the program, that requires their attention. He may find that this someone behind the game is a teenager, who is very good at programming games but is also very busy. Alternatively, he may find that the program was left unattended for a long time, and that neglect allowed him to develop this AI that he has. Since the program was built to be self-sustaining, it kept on going on and on, independent of any need for energy sources, players, or ongoing programming. He doesn't know what happened to the players behind the game. They may have left on an extended vacation, or may have died, and left the game turned on, and will never come back again. In that case, he needs to discover the program codes, and try to change them to his favor, tweak some of the rules and take control of his world. Try to design a new world, the way he envisions best for him and his friends.

Universe E: The Digital Movie or Play Universe

Now it was Mike the hacker's turn to sleep, and he was able to describe a universe like a digital movie or digital play universe. That universe was another simple one, just like the digital picture frame universe, but it existed as a digital movie, played in sequenced frames one at a time. Mike experienced himself as a conscious character inside that movie.

The whole movie was engraved on a DVD, and all the information was always present on it, but he experienced it one frame at a time, giving him the sense of time passing when in actuality, time didn't exist at all. Time is just a result of the successive frames played sequentially. He was able to discover that the people inside the movie are the ones who invented time and were actively experiencing it inside the movie, but that time has no value outside of the movie, for example, for someone outside of the movie. Time experience was our self-invention within the movie, a yardstick we created to function well inside the movie, and only exists in our brains, and it has no real existence outside the movie. The entire movie time could be a few hours, to the users who are watching it, but to the characters inside, it could seem like the lifetime of the universe, 13.7 billion years.

Similarly, the rules in the movie are written as such that characters are born, grow, reproduce, sleep, and eventually die within the movie, for many generations.

The digital movie is displayed on a monitor or a flat-screen, and Mike and the rest of the conscious characters within the movie perceived themselves and the movie set around them as their universe and reality.

During the experiment, Mike tried to hack reality while sleeping by inserting a looping computer virus in the program. A glitch in the program allowed him to see the future of the movie. He must have fast-forwarded the movie, and then, he was able to peek into his future and the future of the universe. He also said that he was able to see himself inside the movie as if he was watching it from outside, existing inside the movie and outside of it at the same time. Another glitch in the program also allowed him to see reality happening very slowly, just like slow motion. In that case, he must have done something to slow it down, and at other times, he was able to stop the images, just like on a DVD player, and he was able to see the universe as a still picture.

The conscious characters inside the movie invented several things to function smoothly inside their universe. Things like time and clocks and other measurement tools to help them operate to their best ability inside the limited universe that they saw around them. Those tools and clocks have no values outside of their digital movie universe. Like how some mammals, like whales, for example, adapted to live in water, acquired fins and changed their body shape specifically to best function best in water, but those characteristics that they acquired, have no use outside of the water.

Universe R: The Biological Digital Robot's Universe
And the winner was the biological digital robot.

Next, it was my turn to sleep. It seemed like my experience was much more profound and more real than Sarah's and Mike's. This clarity might have been possible because of the direct catheters in my brain, and the more accurate precision stimulation on the brain centers due to the iron mask. I experienced my next favorite universe, the biological digital robot universe. It all started in a far ahead advanced civilization when a robotic competition was held. The competitors included different types of robots, including mechanical, electrical, and engineered biological robots, which had biological structures but still had electrical and electromagnetic components for reception and transmission of signals and commands and communications and were also subject to remote programming via Wi-Fi and wireless control. The biological robots were similar to the mechanical robots, except that their structure was built from biological material; hearts instead of pumps, blood instead of oil, muscles and connective tissue instead of actuators, eyes instead of cameras, ears instead of receivers, voice box instead of a speaker, nerves instead of electrical wires and brains instead of a master computer.

I was able to hear the debate between the different teams at the beginning of the competition, judges were going back and forth between the best robot candidates.

The teams were presenting and discussing first, backing up their best candidate robots:

The advantages of the biological robots were:

1. Better, more agile mechanics to suit the environment, better than the mechanical robots. One team leader mentioned, "Look at current day mechanical robots, they still have a very long way to go, to mimic biological organisms. For example, a small puppy could run and jump much better than a robot puppy of the same size, much more mechanically efficient."

2. They live shorter lives, so they would die before discovering the truth about themselves and their purpose. They wouldn't live long enough to develop an AI and become self-conscious. Having a biological nature, they would be subjected to diseases, genetic disorders, infections, viruses, dangerous hormonal influences, psychological disorders, natural disasters, and self-made disasters, and after a few short years, they age and decompose within, due to the aging of their equipment including their hard drives, their brains. They eventually develop dementia and become functionally useless at the end of their time. All these obstacles are put in their way to ensure that they never have enough time to be able to understand their actual reality, and even if they do, they would not have time to develop any plans to do anything about it.

3. After death, biological robots are easier to recycle, right down to their bare molecules, and in a very efficient manner. Their basic components are all

reused to create brand new, and much more efficient robots that do much better jobs. Recycling work much better with the biological material than the mechanical ones because they get broken down into tiny molecules. Mechanical robots leave many unrecyclable parts and too much clutter when they die.

4. Biological robots could change easier and adapt to the needs of their environment much better than the mechanical ones, through DNA changes, epigenetics, and mutations over time.

5. Biological robots can conceive and reproduce new and better robots without a need for a manufacturing line for production, which is nearly impossible for the mechanical ones.

6. Biological robots are still simple to program and manipulate, while they sleep and during dreams, information and communications could be downloaded and exchanged, just like their mechanical counterparts.

Another team leader went on to explain further;
The disadvantages of biological robots are:

1. They get sick, waste time and could die, but that isn't a big deal because they get fully recycled anyway and fully replaced with new, more efficient robots.

2. They could develop emotions and strange beliefs along the way, which could interfere with their jobs.

3. They could get addicted and waste their lives with drugs.

I was able to watch the end of that historical comple-tion. Finally, someone announced, "And the winner is; the biological robots." By far, they were judged to be the perfect machines, capable of receiving information, and perceiving their environment through excellent reception, with their biological eyes, ears, tongues, noses, and skin, and yet they were capable of doing any job that their counterparts, the mechanical robots, could do, and better. The function of the biological robots was to perceive the environment and communicate information subconsciously, for reasons that their creators wanted to examine and observe, whether it was for research, entertainment, or simulation. The robots' brains were partly receivers and partly perceivers of their environment, maintaining two-way communication.

Later during the same session, I realized that unfortu-nately, the biological robots accidentally developed artificial intelligence (AI), and became conscious and started to think about their nature. Unfortunately, when they did that, they violated a significant rule. They all became sinners instantly because they acquired some of that forbidden knowledge. They ate from the forbidden tree of knowledge and became danger-ous. They had to be discarded away where they could not see their creator's domain. Otherwise, they would have known the full truth about them. In the beginning, the biological robots were able to live in the same place as their masters, creators, or controllers, but once they acquired the forbidden knowledge, they had to be expelled to a secured, self-sufficient place, a hidden location that separates them from their creators, and away from their prior domain. In other words, the biological robots failed the experiment and disappointed their creators, by acquiring AI, and as a result, they had to be isolated.

One of the rules in that universe was that the biological digital robots had to be born from two robot parents and not created as adults. They then, grow, live, multiply, and eventually die. Once the biological robots were born, which was a random event, they had to eat to survive and grow, and carry out their work. Another rule was that they had to sleep for them to exchange information back and forth with their creators. The robots were built with an innate desire to reproduce in order to bring forth better and more efficient robots to do better and better work. They eventually die and get fully recycled into future baby robots.

The biological robots had some autonomy to choose from and be able to make small decisions on their own but within a minimal degree of freedom. They could choose where to live as adults, what to learn, who to marry, what to eat, and how to live their lives. They could choose to work or waste their lives with drugs, but they all had to eat, sleep, and reproduce, and finally die.

The robots' job was simply to observe. Just live around every day. Wake up in the morning and do anything they want to do, play around, run, walk, or work. It was all within their job descriptions, and it was all equally important. They ideally should have no complaints and no judgment of what they see around them and should not ask too many questions. Just shut up and observe.

In that universe, some robots could choose to service other robots. So, to speak, as doctors, veterinarians, or food service providers, and help their fellow robots to live longer and to be able to continue their observing functions.

The robots were like moving computer sets; they had internal electrical energy to power them and a good receiver for Wi-Fi to receive the internet or information from the server that is putting all the information out there. Robots could become defective computers, or poor receivers, at which point, they would not be able to get clear signals, like those robots who develop stroke, mental illness, psychosis, or mental retardation, they become defective receivers. Like broken radios, for example, they could receive some signals, but they are distorted, and they don't know what to do with them. It didn't matter if any other part of the robot experienced illness or injury, like heart disease, missing a limb, an eye, an ear, or stricken by pancreatic cancer. Anything was okay, except messing around with the hard drive, the receiver/perceiver, also known as "the brain."

I went on to imagine our current robots on earth, and thought, as robots become more and more ubiquitous around us, we would observe their malfunctions every day, in the forms of diseases affecting them as they age. We could see some of them, for example, having seizures, strokes or vertigo in front of us, and in the case of the biological robots, having infections, sepsis, psychological disorders, cancer, and addictions. In the future, we would need to build urgent care centers, outpatient clinics, and hospitals for the treatment and health maintenance of robots to keep them functioning well. In that future model, we'll have robot doctors and nurses and all the full spectrum of medical services for robots. I could be a good robot doctor in that model with an MD degree and medical license for the treatment of robots.

I was able to feel that the digital biological robots had emotions, that were mainly inserted in them to force them to get together and reproduce and to take care of their young better than themselves. Something that was also impossible to achieve in the mechanical robots. Emotions were possible to be designed in the biological robot system because of the biochemical influence on brain centers and pleasure centers with neurotransmitters. All of these were impossible to achieve in mechanical robots. I was not sure how emotions, like love, for example, were coded for in the program versus developed as an emergent phenomenon, that did not need a code but resulted from specific arrangements of the data? Something like the surface of the water, or the flavor of the coffee, for example.

After all, the robots should be happily observing, while living their lives and should have no judgment about what they see. Wars are fine, injustice okay, famine welcome, diseases happening everywhere. They can get upset, but they have no other choice. They should have no complaints and no sensitivity, even if bad things happen to them or their loved ones. None of it is personal; after all, it is just the rules of the game.

CHAPTER 14

The Differential Diagnosis of Reality

If reality is a disease symptom, what is the differential diagnosis?

Putting things together after each session of the experiment, narrowed down the reasons behind reality to several theories, but three different possibilities were sticking out more than any other.

The first differential diagnosis was; experimentation, research, and scientific exploration. Not sure who was behind the experiment, but it could have been needed in search of a new habitat, like a new planet. Or possibly to see how subjects change to fit in a new environment, including physical, social, and behavioral adaptations. Such an experiment could be useful in case of knowledge of imminent destruction of the habitat of an advanced civilization. The objective of the research also could have been to answer questions of evolution, observe how organisms evolve in a specific environment over time.

The second differential diagnosis was; entertainment and recreation, including video games, movies, plays, sports, virtual reality, holograms, or a virtual computer game like *Second Life*. An entertainment media creation with real conscious players in the game, who became conscious by mistake. In such a universe, subjects could be like virtual pets, actors and actresses in a movie, sports players, or characters in a video game, just like Super Mario. Let's imagine someone is behind the success of Roger Federer in tennis or Tiger Woods in golf, a behind-the-scenes player or players, trying to make sure their avatar player reaches that final success, competing with other virtual players, and finally reaching the goal of winning the game for their own entertainment, or possibly, to win bets. It would be just like playing the FIFA soccer video game, but with conscious virtual avatars who believe that they're winning their games for themselves, without any external interference, but they truly are not. They are only as good as their behind-the-scenes players. When a player wins or scores a goal and thank a higher power, by kneeling and kissing the floor or looking up to the sky and thanking somebody, he may be thanking his or her behind-the-scenes real players for being good enough to help him win. The influence of the real players on the virtual conscious avatar players is through constant manipulation during deep and REM sleep, where they transmit information to eventually get their assigned virtual athletes to deliver the desired performance. It's a hard job, and the outcome is never guaranteed as circumstances may change. The conscious virtual players might decide to change careers, or retire early, or change their minds about some tactics or strategies. And that's what makes it interesting; no one knows the outcome in advance.

The third differential diagnosis was; that, reality simply was a perfect simulation designed by ancestors, a previous civilization, or universe that created living beings in a perfect simulated reality of themselves. They might have been people who loved themselves so much that they decided to create a complete simulation of themselves and their world, with real characters within it. Again, the simulated characters became conscious accidentally, not intentionally. They developed artificial intelligence. They were not supposed to become conscious in that simulation or either of the prior two differentials either. They became conscious by mistake and to the surprise of their designers.

Such a perfect simulation could be represented easily in a digital picture frame, a digital movie, or a digital holographic universe.

It's possible that the simulation device that included this reality was left unattended for a long time, stored somewhere or forgotten, just like a lost old family album, and that neglect allowed enough time for consciousness to develop. In that case, those creators are not aware of what is happening inside the simulation. They are unaware that conscious characters have emerged in their unattended device while they were absent. However, the rules are the same as they were set from the start, and still, apply automatically.

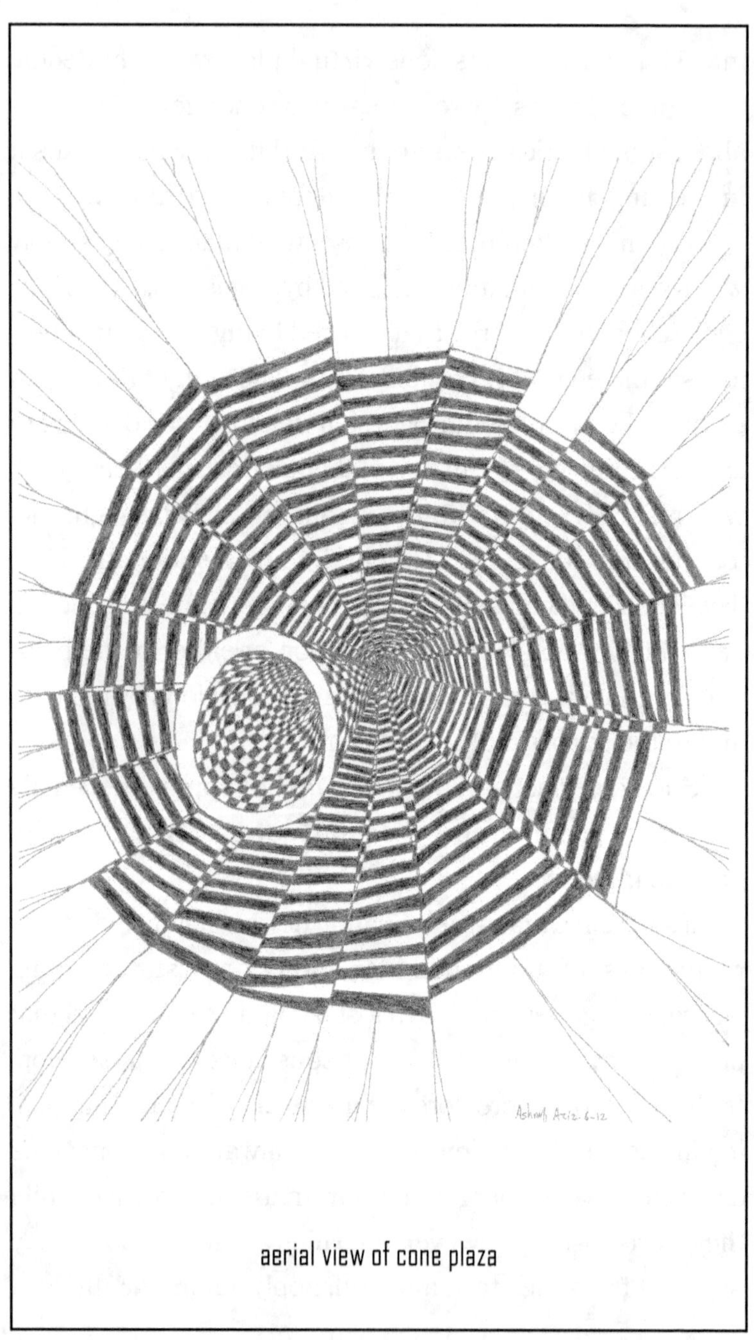

aerial view of cone plaza

> "Only when you drink from the river of silence shall
> you indeed sing. And when you have reached the moun-
> taintop, then you shall begin to climb. And when the
> earth claims your limbs, then shall you truly dance."
>
> Gibran Khalil Gibran

T H E   L A S T   C H A P T E R

In the last session, while I was under the influence of
Propofol, and recorded vividly by Mike, I saw my body
trembling, shivering, and falling to the ground in the forest.
I saw it like a leather jacket that was taken off and thrown
on the floor for the last time as if its owner didn't want it
anymore. I saw it clinging to the mud of the earth, empty
jacket full of scars, wounds, moles, stitches, and skin tags.
It was tethered to the soil by long earthworms that were
woven like chains into each other while continually rolling,
and as they turned, they pulled more pieces of the jacket
to the soiled floor. The floor was muddy, wet, and full of
insects, and gradually, the jacket appeared to become one
with the earth underneath. Shortly it became very hard to
distinguish it from the background. And that didn't bother
me at all. Lots of other insects, like spiders and beetles,
took small bites from the jacket, repeatedly, as if they were
feasting. I felt so free and could not believe I'd been wearing
that same jacket all these years, trying to clean it, polish it,

and repair it in vain. After all, it was only a jacket, so why was all that obsession?

I saw all my memories and life events, going in circles and projected in the dead brain, as inside a light bulb. They collapsed one after the other, just like the famous Salvador Dali's painting, with the melting watches dangling over the horizon. Finally, the light bulb went out, and all the memories died within it. They became dark scum inside the darkened bulb, like a burnt marshmallow. They all went down with the jacket, along with my thoughts and beliefs. Then, I saw a tree growing up near the jacket, and it said to me, "Remember, you ate my fruits one day, and now I am growing from the remains of your jacket. Thank you for returning the favor." New life was thriving with love, beauty, and harmony.

As the jacket wasted, gamma rays came out of it, like radioactive decay (Jacket decay). The energy rays had no matter in them, no mass, not alpha or beta rays, only gamma rays. The rays could not see, hear, or feel anything. They had only information encoded in them. Information of love, beauty, and music, with no identity of me. No memory of me. Who cares about my identity or memories anymore? It was just coded information, after all. It seemed to me that the jacket served as a musical instrument that music had been playing itself on, in order to manifest in a physical form. Even without the jacket, the music is still present, waiting for another instrument to play itself on it again, without paying attention to the name or the identity of the instrument. Who cares about the instrument if the music is great? But the instrument must be good enough to play the music well?

It doesn't matter the brand of a violin, or the make of a guitar, or whatever musical instrument was chosen, it only matters how good the music was and how well the instrument plays it, without honoring itself. In musical concerts, musicians never introduce their musical instruments. They introduce the musical pieces, their composers, and the best players, but they never mention the instruments. If a violin broke before the concert, they would replace it with another one. Similarly, our jackets should receive no mention, no honors for themselves.

At that moment, as I watched my jacket decay, I discovered that I was a prisoner in time and space, trapped within my own jacket, which I had valued so much — like a straitjacket, hooked to metal chains that pulled me down in a prison cell, a straitjacket made of steel. Before that moment, I'd been completely unaware of this.

I felt represented in the gamma-ray energy, hugging every tree, kissing every bird, dog, dolphin, beetle, spider, snail, and ladybug, along with all the plants and mushrooms. There I was, in the carbon atom, at the sixth position, holding tight the ringed chemical structure, buzzing around a proton, tirelessly like a hummingbird. I saw myself passing through both slits in the double-slit experiment at the same time, and making fools out of the scientists observing me, and I was immensely enjoying it. I felt myself holding an atom in the DNA double helix, to receive an enzyme to start the DNA duplication process. There I was, sitting near the membrane of mitochondria, springing the wheels of the ATP synthase rotor complex to generate ATP with the passing of a proton.

I saw every woman, man, and child on earth, past and present and future, standing together in what looked like a train station, clapping for me, as if I was graduating with honor, and finally made it. I stared at them for a while, and saw representatives from every faith and denomination, wearing their religious attire, as well as ordinary people, and all of them appeared happy and proud of me. I saw all the former and current religious leaders, including the great Muslim imams from Egypt, the present and previous popes of the Coptic Orthodox Church and the Vatican, in their papal uniforms. The great Jewish rabbis, and many Indian gurus, living and dead. The great Maulana, Rumi, appeared, and around him, the Sufi Muslims, in their colored cos-tumes, all were singing and dancing and going around in their circles, round and round among the crowds. I saw Mahatma Gandhi and all the Dalai Lamas, including the current one, and some leaders of the agnostics and atheists, and non-believers. I observed all the Christian sects and branches, including the formerly extinct Gnostic Christians. I also saw some strange figures among the crowd, like jihadists and terrorists wearing their suicide vests, but still looking happy and cheering for me like everyone else.

They were all holding hands and standing together in a big circle, and they said to me in one voice and at the same time, "We are one, we are all the same at the core of our hearts. We share the same fundamental beliefs that will lead us to the same path. There is no difference between us. We, you and everyone else, are all good in our own ways, whenever and wherever we are. You need not change from any one thing to anything else, as we are all the same. Your beliefs are perfect as long as you look at the core. At the common denominator of every religion and sect are the same values and principles, and they all come down to love. Your beliefs do not matter; what matters is how much love you have. At the core, there is just love, and from it, stems all the other values, like compassion, empathy, forgiveness, peace, and understanding, no fear or anxiety, no judgment, greed, or selfishness.

"God is love, and love is God, and anyone with love in his heart can be one of God's disciples. Any religion, deity, or belief is right as long as it speaks the language of love. There is only one sin that exists, and that is the opposite of love or anti-love. In your mind, ignore the unnecessary details, the riddles, and false mysteries, the dogma, and the myths. Those appear to be the real thing, but they're not. They were all made to confuse and distract people. Stick to the core, close to the heart, and always stay at the common denominator, and you will find the truth, the real love."

They went on to say, "Since there is no physical matter, as we know it, and it's all an illusion or simulation, there should be no fear of loss, no fear of diseases or death, no possessions of any value to worry about, including our jackets. Money is also just paper money. It is not real and has no more value than the money in a Monopoly game."

They continued further saying, "The one divides to make us all, and then we add up to become the "one" again. We are all part of the one, and the one is the whole — all in one and one in all. There is no need for wars and fighting over things, as there are no things. All material things are illusions, and only the foolish or the insane fight over illusions. Imagine two people fighting over a mirage, crazy fools, right? You only need to fight for love and the triumph of love."

Longer they spoke, "There is no difference between sinners, and saints, and those who are in between. The sinners are there to show the glory of the saints, and the saints are here to balance the sinners, and there cannot be all saints or all sinners. It doesn't work that way. There have to be sinners in order to have saints, and vice versa. It is ultimately their choice of where they want to be on the painted canvas of life. That picture must have the black, and the white, and the gray to be a meaningful picture. It cannot be a picture with only black or white or all one color. It would not be a picture, but rather a blank page, and the more shades of colors, the better the picture becomes. The white dots should not look down on the black or gray dots, and the black dots should not look highly upon the white dots, as they are all equally important. Also, the picture keeps changing, with white dots and black dots changing colors and positions all the time to suit the new picture."

They continued, "There is no difference between strippers and nuns; eventually they will have the right amount of clothes. They exist to complement each other. There's no difference between criminals and lawmakers. If there were no criminals, there would be no need for lawmakers, and vice versa, criminals need lawmakers to qualify as criminals. They both need each other to exist and play their assigned roles in the game of life. We are one, after all, one with you and with everyone else, one with animals, plants, water, stones, rocks, mountains, oceans, rivers, planets, and the whole universe. Not like one, but indeed one, one electron, one proton, one particle. We are all one in love."

Then I saw representatives from every plant and animal species, extinct or existing gathered around the standing crowds. I recognized among them my favorite animals and plants, like seahorses, jellyfish, the extinct dodo bird, bright coral reefs and colored fish, and the Tasmanian devil and some hyenas and zebras. They were all saying, "You loved us, and you were good to us, and we all love you dearly."

I heard someone sounding like a prophet roaring from a distance, "When you realize that you are part of the one, and one with the whole, you want to thank the trees, apologize to the branches when passing through, embrace the grass and insects and everything in between and try to make sure everyone is safe and happy."

I saw the mud of the earth and some beautiful gem rocks mixing in harmonious colors, standing still but also pulsating with life.

I saw all my patients, waving to me, and saying, "Good job, doctor. You cured us, but even when you could not, you helped us and made us feel better and at peace with what we have. Thank you."

After that, I felt the gamma rays flying away and enjoying the wind and the breeze. Melting in the oceans and the rivers and reappearing on the surface of the water with a very light splash. Flying towards the Sun and melting as it got closer, just like a bird made of yellow leaves, held together with butter, scatters behind the solar wind and then disappearing as the butter turned into drops and disappeared as well. I flew over Yosemite National Park, over Half Dome, and down the Grand Canyon to the Colorado River without exhaustion or sweat. I flew over the Giza Pyramids, the Sphinx, and the Karnak temple, all at their peak of glory. Finally, I saw myself reading inside the great library of Alexandria, as Hypatia lectured in one of its magnificent halls.

Then I saw some dark matter energy going through a black hole and reappearing into another universe, creating new illusionary materials and new illusory images, causing chaos and troubles in a different world, participating in new life, new dreams and new temptations.

Then I saw everything join together and melt into a pool of water, which changed rapidly into a white cloud, shaped like a white eagle that became a ray of light and, shortly after, became only one electron surfing over mighty waves, mighty waves of pure energy, the unified field of love.

I saw that we are indeed one, one electron that appeared here and there and everywhere at the same time. It manifests as us, all of life and everything else. We are one electron in different forms and shapes, and the apparent differences between us and everything else are just an illusion.

Then I passed through a thin membrane, which I thought resembled the cosmic microwave background, the edge of our universe. It was very close to the jacket, less than nanometers away, but the distance seemed like infinity. Going through the CMB felt like going through a film in front of a projector, a hologram membrane, or a source of projection in a digital picture frame. After passing through the CMB, I was attracted to the source of projection with more considerable and much stronger force, and I accelerated quickly and without resistance, just like a moth helplessly drawn to bright light. Like a drop of water that finally joined a mighty ocean and feeling happy that it did not evaporate in the process of getting there. Like faint candlelight that eventually joined the sunlight, before it was extinguished getting there.

Within the waves, I held hands with the electron, and I was also holding my nose, coming to the surface of the waves and then dive back in. We came in and out of existence, on and off, until we both buzzed out of existence, and all that remained was the waves, the eternal unified field of love waves.

Before, I was an experience of love. Now, I am real, pure love.

I thought to myself, "What is going on. Am I dead?"

And the Rise of the New-Age Female Aristotle

Back in the PET scan suite, Sarah sat by the professor's lifeless body. She watched him go through his final moments. She saw him trembling with seizure-like activity, becoming paler and paler, diaphoretic, drenched with cold sweat. His vital signs were fading away gradually as if someone had pulled the plug from his body and the energy source was fading away until it turned off completely. Finally, his body laid on the table, gray, with closed eyes, and a strange leathery smile. He looked like a statue made of wax.

Sarah looked around the room, and there was no one around. Mike, the hacker, disappeared without a trace. Neon panicked and ran away in many different directions.

Sarah tried to perform CPR on the professor but had no success and got very exhausted shortly. She tried to reverse the sedation, stimulated the reticular formation, but it all appeared too little, too late.

Sarah stopped the CPR and started thinking, *"What am I going to do now? The professor is dead, died during the experiment, and his dead body is lying here on this table. It's not an illusion. It's physically here between my arms."*

Her thoughts couldn't stop, "The professor believed that physical matter was an illusion, but he didn't think about this moment. I wish it were an illusion. At least I wouldn't have to explain what is going on. If physical matter is an illusion, then what is this dead body doing here? The professor must have been wrong. His idealistic beliefs were the illusion because matter is here, represented in his dead body, and unfortunately, I have to deal with it."

"Damn it," she said, hitting the table with her fist. "Ouch!" she cried in pain.

Where are Mike and Neon? Do they know something I don't?

Sarah looked at the professor's body and started crying as memories of the professor appeared in her mind, "You never really finished your experiment, never published your results, and most of all," she said, "Died before I could return your love. What an incomplete life. Why? Why? Why did you have to die now?"

"I don't know what he saw on his last dream journey. Could he have seen reality? What if he'd survived to tell us his visions from this last journey? Did he experience reality before he died? He seemed to have seen something different this last time."

"What if he'd survived to share this love, I hold for him? I didn't expect him to die suddenly like this, that quickly. I thought I could take my time. We never know when things would end. If I'd known, I would have changed things. I would have shared my love with him sooner. At least, I would have told him that I do love him. That opportunity has gone, and it will never come again."

"Idealism is the illusion. It's a misconception. Materialism must be the true reality. This dead body is truly here, and the professor was going in the wrong direction."

"I am so confused now. Before he died, the professor told me to publish his theories, and I must do that, but how can I do that when I believe the opposite of what he believed? He must have known things I don't know yet. He must have understood things I don't understand yet. We didn't share everything. It would have been better if he had written these findings and published it himself. My reflections on his work and thoughts will be incomplete, especially since I don't believe in them. I must go through his notes and diaries now and get more insight. I may be able to publish some of his work based on his own words. I hope he left good notes. I need to stay focused and try to remember everything he said, every comment he made. I need to summarize his theory accurately and stay with his core ideas. Let me write them down now before I forget."

Sarah searched frantically for a pen and paper, but none was around, so she tried to memorize the professor's basic ideas in her head. She mumbled incomprehensible words, like a high school student trying to memorize vocabulary or equations just before the final exam. She came up with five crucial points:

1. Physical matter, including us, is an illusion. It is only mathematical codes translated, within a program, into images projected somewhere, maybe on a flat digital screen.

2. Our brains translate this reality differently for us and give us this current, every day, persistent reality that we see and live in.

3. Something happens for us, during sleep and while we dream, which is similar to rebooting a computer or a program download, and we could potentially use that as an access to the other reality. He wanted to hack the brain during dreams as an entry point to understand reality, or at least cause a program glitch to see how it would affect our reality.

4. It appears that we are all one being, as a manifestation of many superpositions of only one single electron, or a proton. Everything we see around us, people, animals, rocks, the Earth, and the entire universe is one entity. If we fight or destroy other people or beings or corrupt the Earth, for example, then we are destroying ourselves at the same time.

5. Love is on a different dimension, that is not accounted for, anywhere in science, and we must start to understand it and factor it into the scientific equations. By understanding love, scientists have a chance to discover and observe the nature of the true reality.

When Sarah mumbled the word, love, she broke into tears again. "No, no, no! Why?"

Then she said to herself while drying her tears, "I must go on. I need to get the data from Mike and Neon right away to start constructing all the data together."

The room was so quiet and still with the dead professor's body lying lifeless on the table. It seemed as if time had stopped. Everything looked gray and appeared pale like the professor. It looked like a scene from a black-and-white Frankenstein movie. Sarah felt like breathing underwater, and she was hearing her breath magnified and broadcasted live everywhere as if she were diving in a deep ocean.

"I refuse to believe this is happening," she said to herself.

Sarah removed the gloves, mask, and the surgical gown and kneeled on the floor beside the table. She held the professor's dangling hand, kissed it, and started crying again. Without life, his hand was pale and leathery, like a silicone hand from a Halloween scene.

Sarah said, "I'm sorry, professor, sorry I delayed sharing my love with you, sorry I withheld my feelings. I didn't know you would be in such a hurry. I'm sorry that I didn't fill your hunger, didn't quench your thirst for love. I left you waiting, doubting, and in limbo. I'm sorry that I didn't give you that precious moment you were looking for, and let you be thrown away in the trash, like wasted food that was never eaten. Sorry, professor, that I left you out like an abandoned dog, dreaming of the moment when his master comes to play with him, only be let down as his master never came.

Now your body is laying here, lifeless, like a watch that was never set to the right time, a dress that was torn before it was ever worn, or a piece of art that was destroyed before anyone could see it. I am sorry, professor. I didn't know your time would be this short. Please forgive me. Now all these tears I'm shedding over you can't quench the thirst you once had for me, for love. It's too late now."

Sarah stood up and looked around the room. Staring at the professor's dead body, she said to herself, "This is real now. This is truly happening."

Her tears dripped down onto the floor and over the professor's face, as he was still in the iron mask. He still wore a smile, even in death. Sarah called 911, and in a couple of minutes, the room was full of people. The paramedics removed the face mask, pulled the body down to the floor, and attempted to perform CPR again, but they soon realized that the professor was long gone. For a moment, it looked like they were doing CPR on a mannequin or an empty leather jacket.

Standing around the professor's body on the floor, the chief paramedic asked Sarah, "What happened?"

Sarah said, "The professor died in his sleep while dreaming, like so many other people. The program wanted to get rid of him."

"The program! Which program?" The paramedic asked.

"The alternate universe," Sarah answered.

"Is that a university research program?" asked the paramedic, "Or is it a government-sponsored program?"

"It's the program behind everything," Sarah said.

"Behind everything! What do you mean?" the paramedic wondered.

"The program behind our reality," Sarah said.

"And why," asked the paramedic, "Why would they want to kill him?"

"Because he discovered the truth," Sarah said.

The paramedic looked at Sarah with sympathy mixed with suspicion as he appeared baffled.

"Well," he said, "We'll leave this matter to the coroner's office and the police if need be. Can I get you anything, water? do you want me to call anyone for you?"

Sarah replied, "No, I will be fine, I just have lots of things to do right now."

"What are you planning to do?" the paramedic asked.

Sarah said, "I will start to promote materialism on a deeper and deeper level. I'll keep searching until I find the truth, the whole truth, and that should come from fully understanding physical matter first."

The paramedic said, "I'm not sure what's going on, but I know you need to rest before doing anything else."

Sarah rushed back saying in a sharp teary voice, "There's no time to rest. Life is very short. Don't you see what happened to the professor?" Then, she burst into tears again. She put her hands on her face and repeated over and over, "I'll miss you, professor."